Introducing Miss Joanna

Once a Wallflower
Book Two

Maggi Andersen

ARE YOU SIGNED UP FOR DRAGONBLADE'S BLOG?

You'll get the latest news and information on exclusive giveaways, exclusive excerpts, coming releases, sales, free books, cover reveals and more.

Check out our complete list of authors, too!

No spam, no junk. That's a promise!

Sign Up Here

www.dragonbladepublishing.com

Dearest Reader;

Thank you for your support of a small press. At Dragonblade Publishing, we strive to bring you the highest quality Historical Romance from the some of the best authors in the business. Without your support, there is no 'us', so we sincerely hope you adore these stories and find some new favorite authors along the way.

Happy Reading!

CEO, Dragonblade Publishing

Additional Dragonblade books by Author Maggi Andersen

The Never Series
Never Doubt a Duke
Never Dance with a Marquess
Never Trust and Earl

Dangerous Lords Series
The Baron's Betrothal
Seducing the Earl
The Viscount's Widowed Lady
Governess to the Duke's Heir
Eleanor Fitzherbert's Christmas Miracle (A Novella)

Once a Wallflower Series
Presenting Miss Letitia
Introducing Miss Joanna

The Lyon's Den Connected World
The Scandalous Lyon

Also from Maggi Andersen
The Marquess Meets His Match
Beth

Introducing Miss Joanna

She's hoping to find true love.

He prefers to remain single and bring criminals to justice.

When a dangerous gang threatens her life, his heart is on the line.

London, 1817

WHEN JOANNA DALRYMPLE'S father inherits a fortune from a relative, he sells his haberdashery and turns his attention to seeing his beloved daughter settled in the manner he'd promised her mother. He leases a townhouse in Mayfair for the Season and engages a lady to ease their way into Society.

At her first ball, Jo makes a new friend, Letitia Cartwright, who introduces her to the baron, Lord Reade. Dark-haired and handsome, he towers over most men, and his teasing manner is not what one finds on a ballroom dance floor. Jo learns from Letty that Reade is not looking to marry. It intrigues Jo. There is something mysterious about the baron. An air of danger surrounds him. But Jo has decided her husband must be a quiet gentleman who would welcome her widowed father into their house, so when the elegant Mr. Ollerton, pursues her, Jo welcomes his advances.

Gareth Baron Reade, an agent for the crown, is investigating the disappearances of several young women at the request of the Prince Regent. The lovely redhead, Miss Joanna Dalrymple, has captured Reade's attention. His interest in her deepens.

His good friend, Brandon Cartwright, has the annoying tendency to read Reade's mind, and to voice what's on his. He urges Reade to marry and cast aside the low spirits which have plagued him since Waterloo. But Reade refuses to inflict his dark moods and nightmares on a wife. Trouble is, Joanna, a forthright young woman, becomes increasingly difficult to ignore. Especially when it appears she might be in danger.

Has she become involved with the Virdens, the couple Reade has under suspicion? While he has no intention of caring for anyone again, he becomes determined to protect her.

Will it take a matter of life and death for them to realize they cannot live without each other?

CHAPTER ONE

Marlborough, Wiltshire
March 1817

"IT'S SOLD!"

Joanna Dalrymple's father burst through the door, his face wreathed in smiles. She glanced up from slicing meat for their luncheon at the kitchen table. Their maid, Molly, left her seat, and transferring the bowl of shelled peas to the sideboard, withdrew from the room.

"That is wonderful news, Papa."

"Not surprising, as the haberdashery is a neat little business." He brushed a hand over his faded red locks and sat down. "An excellent position, Marlborough being a market town on the Bath Road, it gets all the traffic from London to Bath. Not to mention the shop is on the second-widest high street in Britain, after Stockton-on-Tees."

"Yes, Papa." While Jo had heard it all before, she was glad her father no longer had to work so hard after he inherited money from a relative who'd done extremely well in the silk business at Spitalfields and invested wisely. Papa was now a man of leisure, but unused to idleness, he still cast around for something to occupy his days.

"Are you pleased the shop has sold?"

"I am." He sawed through a loaf of bread with the bread knife and spread butter on two slices. "It's an excellent time to sell, now with the taxes Pitt has imposed. My best lines, including tea, sugar, soap, candles, and paper, are all heavily taxed because of the enormous national debt. The Corn Laws protect the landowners, so the rich grow richer, and the poor grow poorer." He placed a slice of ham on the bread.

Jo passed him the mustard. She wondered if he would ever accept he was now a wealthy man. "You could own a farm again. Employ men to do the hard work."

"And I might one day. But now I have a surprise." His enthusiasm reminded her of their dog, Sooty, after he'd hidden his bone under the sofa cushion.

"A surprise?" Jo grinned as she poured him a cup of tea from the kitchen's brown china teapot.

"I engaged a business manager to find us a house in London for the Season."

"London!" Jo squealed. "Papa! How did you manage to keep this from me?"

He folded his arms with a smug smile. "I signed the lease this morning!"

"You did?" Jo couldn't believe her father would do such a thing. Since her mother died, he disliked disruption of any kind and often lectured her that she was too compulsive, and her desire for adventure was unwise. She felt like pinching herself to make sure she wasn't dreaming.

"You shall have your debut as your mother would have wished." A shadow appeared in his green eyes. "I promised her you would have your chance, and here you are at twenty-one. The men you meet at assemblies and church dances are not good enough for my girl. Your mother married beneath her when she chose me, bless her heart. I pray I never gave her cause to regret it." He sighed. "While I dislike your mother's family, and what they did to Mary, throwing her out because she took your mother's side, I have to admit they are well-born."

"A Season? I can't believe it," Jo said, slightly breathless. "Is Aunt Mary to come with us?"

"Your aunt complains of her rheumatism but expresses an eagerness to accompany us."

"She will enjoy being among society people again."

"I believe she will. I have promised to purchase that cottage your aunt wants. She intends to move there with her cats after you marry."

"She has had her eye on that cottage for ages." While she was pleased for Aunt Mary, Jo felt a quiver of unease. Should she marry, her father would be alone here. He must come and live with her. And any man she married would need an agreeable nature. Someone calm, gentle, and kind.

Her father fed a piece of meat to Sooty, patiently waiting at his feet. "Where is your aunt?"

"She has taken an apple pie to Mrs. Jones, who's feeling poorly." Jo jumped up. "When do we leave? I must make a list."

"Now, I don't intend to leave immediately! There is much to do to prepare. You have need of a ballgown."

"We can purchase it in London," Jo said, fearing something might occur to change his mind.

"Yes. Everything you need, Jo, don't stint on it. But as to the ballgown, you have nothing to worry about, my girl. I have the matter well in hand."

"Oh?" she asked uneasily. Her initial excitement dimmed a little when it occurred to her she was about to be thrown into the midst of Society matrons and their debutante daughters.

"I've spoken to the seamstress, Mrs. Laverty. She has agreed to make your ballgown."

"That is good of her." The widow, Mrs. Laverty, played piquet with her father every Saturday. Jo had hoped they might marry, but her father still mourned her mother.

Mrs. Laverty sewed beautifully but lacked the experience of the London fashions. Jo would study the illustrations in the fashion magazines, but the latest editions weren't easy to get.

"We'll depart for London in April," her father said. "Fred Manion has offered us a ride when next he takes his produce to Covent Garden."

Jo stared at him in surprise. "In his wagon?"

He chuckled. "Heaven forbid! Fred has been doing well and has purchased a carriage to visit his family in Bath. He will be our coachman, while his son, Henry, will drive the vegetable wagon to market."

Jo couldn't help smiling. Her father could well afford a new carriage and a set of prime carriage horses, but she would not dampen his enthusiasm by suggesting it. Especially as she would need a new wardrobe. She'd heard women changed their clothes several times a day in London. Goodness, what an expense!

Some hours later, after she, her father, and Aunt Mary had all contributed their ideas for the trip, Jo retired to her bedchamber to go through her wardrobe. As she feared, nothing was suitable. One wasn't so fussed with what one wore in the country. She tramped for miles over the fields, in good weather and bad, and her half-boots were scuffed, her pelisse faded, and her best poke bonnet, which was perfectly good for church, had seen better days. The subtle differences between a walking dress and a morning dress or an evening gown and a ballgown escaped her. Accessories were a complete mystery. She had no idea which hats and which gloves to wear with what.

Preparing for bed, Jo flicked her braid back and leaned close to her bedchamber mirror. She pondered whether to take the scissors to her waist-length, dark red hair, but decided it needed to be stylishly cut. Her father always said it was her crowning glory, but none of the women passing through the village wore a huge bun at the back of their heads.

During the following weeks, Mrs. Laverty took her measurements and hunted for the right fabric. Jo, eager to see the ballgown, had given the dressmaker an illustration from a magazine she'd found. It was of a slender lady with impossibly tiny feet in a high-waisted dress. Nothing about Jo was tiny. She was tall, and her feet were long and slim like the rest of her. The dress had a low scoop neck and three tiers of ruffles around the hem, with more of the rosebuds sewn onto the capped sleeves. The overall effect was dainty and feminine.

At Jo's first fitting, Mrs. Laverty produced the material for the ballgown. "Your father believes green suits you best, and I quite agree, you have lovely eyes." She picked up the fabric from her table and draped it over Jo's shoulder. "Perfect!"

In the long mirror, Jo studied the effect. The blue-green silk was flattering, although she would have preferred the white muslin with the roses. Mrs. Laverty had not only taken her scissors to the silk but had stitched it together and was now slipping it over Jo's head. "There will be the three ruffles at the hem and the short sleeves you asked for," she said.

The seamstress, enthused by the task, had the gown almost completed by the beginning of the third week. Jo was a little disappointed when she tried it on, but it still needed a few finishing touches.

"It's as you described," Mrs. Laverty said, eyeing her carefully. "I couldn't find any silk rosebuds. The camellias are just as pretty, don't you think?"

Large flowers decorated the hem and smaller ones on the short sleeves. An even bigger camellia sewn onto the skirt made Jo think of a node on a tree. She admitted she was no expert, so decided it would do. And the color was lovely.

"It's beautiful, Mrs. Laverty," she said as the seamstress fussed about with pins in her mouth.

"It does suit you, Jo," Aunt Mary said. "You look wonderful in it."

The day of their departure arrived. Their trunks tied on the back of Fred Manion's carriage, they climbed inside. Fred expressed his satisfaction at having purchased the contraption secondhand at a very good price. The worn seats were hard, and the interior smelled of a sheepdog and something indefinable and unpleasant. However, nothing could rob Jo of excitement as they set out on their journey.

Fred rested the horses at the top of Forest Hill. Then leaving the Wiltshire downs behind them, the carriage rattled on through Savernake Forest, passing tramps, peddlers, and wanderers along the way.

"London, here I come," she said with a grin.

"You will be the belle of the ball," Papa enthused.

"She will." Aunt Mary settled in the corner with several pillows, her eyes shining with anticipation through the lenses of her eyeglasses.

Their first overnight stop was the White Bear at Maidenhead, and without the delays of bad weather, or the need for Fred to use his blunderbuss to ward off highwaymen, they reached Kensington a day later. Their journey was almost at an end. Jo's bottom was sore from the constant jouncing around, and poor Aunt Mary had become pale and silent.

The bustling city was a revelation. Jo stared through the window at the busy streets, the shops, and the dazzling display of wares encroaching on the footpaths. Women boldly strode the street corners and chatted to passing men. The roads were filthy, the gutters overflowing, and coal smoke turned the sky gray. An all-pervasive dank smell rose from the Thames. But none of it mattered. This was London! The carriage pulled up at a crossroads to allow a wagon piled with vegetables to trundle slowly across in front of them.

"They're going to Covent Garden," Fred Manion observed loudly from the box. "That's where I'll be off to as soon as I deposit you in Mayfair."

"So good of you, Fred," Papa yelled back.

"Pies. Pies," a hawker called to them from the pavement. Holding his tray against his chest, supported by a leather strap looped around his neck, he shuffled over to them. "Fancy a beef pie with onions, yer lordship? Ladies? A pastry that fair melts in yer mouth. Made by me missus."

"I'll have one," Fred said, leaning down with a coin in his hand. As he bit into the pie, the gravy must have spilled over his pants. With a curse, the reins slipped from his hands. "No need to worry," he called as he climbed down to retrieve them.

Jo put her head out the window to watch the unfolding scenario with interest.

The pie still clutched in his meaty fingers, Fred was soon up on his box again.

"Eat hearty," the fellow said and bit into the coin before moving back to his position. His cry went up again.

The traffic cleared ahead.

"What are you, top-heavy? Get a move on, you bacon-brained fellow," a groom called from beside the coachman on the box of a glossy black coach.

"Cripes! I'm going, no need to get fidgety," Fred called, waving at them.

Before Fred could move the horses on, the coachman in the black coach took advantage of a gap in the traffic and overtook them.

Halted by another snarl, they stopped side by side. Jo, clutching the window frame, stared directly into the coach and met a gentle-man's dark appraising eyes. His mouth quirked up, and he removed his tall beaver hat, revealing jet-black hair. "Good day," he said through the open window.

She suspected she'd turned scarlet at the amusement in his eyes. "Good day to you, sir," she said crisply.

"Who are you talking to, Jo?" Her father craned his neck to see around her. But the coachman had cracked the whip over the magnificent gray horses and moved the coach on.

Jo's pulse thudded as she gazed after the disappearing coach. "A polite gentleman, Papa."

"Life here is not the same as the country. You must never talk to strange gentlemen in London, Jo," Aunt Mary said, having revived a little at the prospect of the journey's end. "While I was in London as a girl, we couldn't put a foot out the door without the footman."

"Surely times have changed, Aunt Mary," Jo said. She wasn't used to being confined.

Mayfair was different from the parts of the city they'd passed through. Trees lined the clean streets, and some of the houses had gardens. The townhouse her father had leased was one of a row of narrow-fronted ornate brick houses in Upper Brook Street, three-stories plus attic rooms, with fancy ironwork in front. Lord Pleasance, the owner, was traveling on the Continent. His servants came with the house.

Once their carriage had pulled up outside the townhouse, two tall, handsome footmen rushed out. One put down the steps to assist them down, while the other removed their baggage.

Jo joined Aunt Mary and her father to farewell Fred before he drove off to Covent Garden, then they climbed the steps to the glossy black front door, which had an arched window over the top.

A gray-haired butler in black garb waited at the door. He introduced himself as Mr. Spears. Sober faced, he escorted them into the entry where they shed pelisses and hats into the arms of a maid.

Aunt Mary considered it proper to meet the staff, so she and Jo descended below stairs to the servants' quarters to introduce themselves to the cook and the housekeeper. Her aunt was keen to discuss the menus and was quite put out to discover Mrs. Cross, the housekeeper and cook, had the menus for the next week already decided upon. Jo suspected the house ran like clockwork.

Jo's bedchamber was furnished in rose pink and cream floral wallpaper. Sally, the maid who was to attend her, opened the trunk and took out the primrose muslin. Jo cringed to have her few things revealed to the servant's gaze. "I am to have a whole new wardrobe made for the Season."

Sally nodded, her fresh face kind. "There's a bowl of hot water on the dresser, Miss Dalrymple. I'll assist you to change, and shall I tidy your hair?"

Jo put a hand to where hair was escaping the pins and sighed. She must get her hair cut. "Thank you, Sally."

They ate in the dining room at a long table covered in white linen beneath an unlit chandelier. Everything sparkled in the candlelight cast by a pair of silver candelabrum. The footmen served the courses while the butler, Spears, with great aplomb, poured wine from the cellar he'd decanted into crystal glasses. Jo's father added water to Jo's. After the dessert course, which was a delicious syllabub and fruit, her father sat back with a hand on his stomach and instructed Spears to compliment the cook. The butler inclined his head but didn't deem to reply while he poured a glass of port. The man looked down his long nose at her father. Annoyed, Jo held her tongue.

Despite the noisy street below her window, which was so different from the quiet countryside, Jo slept soundly. The next morning after breakfast, while they sat in the parlor making plans for the day, the butler entered carrying a visiting card on a silver salver.

He showed in Mrs. Millet, an attractive, fair-haired woman in her mid-forties, dressed in what Jo considered must be the height of fashion, a spring-green dress and a white straw bonnet trimmed with plaid ribbon and silk flowers. She shook their hands in her gloved one. "How do you do? I trust your journey was satisfactory?"

Jo's father rushed to assure her it was. As he assisted her into a chair, describing their excellent accommodation on the road, Jo covertly studied the woman her father had hired to ease their way in society. She disliked that they must rely on anyone but accepted the necessity for it. The ways of London society were new to them, and she fretted about how well they would be received.

Mrs. Millet's carefully modulated tones lacked warmth, and her smile failed to reach her eyes. Jo supposed she was accustomed to the easy familiarity of country folk, but the lady had exquisite manners.

A maid brought in the tea tray while Mrs. Millet explained how best to begin. It was clear she knew the ins and outs of Society. She explained how Jo must deport herself at a ball and other affairs, discussed her wardrobe and the dressmaker she had engaged to make her clothes, then departed with the promise of securing several invitations from those who agreed to receive them.

They were not top drawer, and could not expect to have an intro everywhere, Mrs. Millet explained at the door with a soothing smile. Whilst Jo considered it unnecessary for her to remind them, there was no getting around it. They were shopkeepers from the country, despite her father's newfound prosperity and her generous dowry.

After the door closed on Mrs. Millet, Jo gave a mental shrug. She wasn't silly enough to set her cap so high as to wish to marry a duke or any titled gentleman. She wanted a man she could love and admire, who accepted her father. Surely, attending all the social engagements Mrs. Millet had mentioned, balls, soirees, breakfasts, and picnics, Jo would meet the man of her dreams and find friends among the other debutantes.

A WHISKY IN his hand, Gareth, Lord Reade, stretched out his legs before the Cartwright's library fire. "It's good to be back in London."

His good friend and colleague, Brandon, strolled over with the crystal decanter to top up Reade's glass. "Your journey didn't go well?"

"Much as I anticipated." He thought of his lonely rambles along the shore, watching the gulls soar over the cold gray waters. "Improvements are continuing at the house."

"Just how bad did your father leave it?"

"He scarcely noticed the decay for some years. Lost heart, I suppose. I never really knew him. As you know, I found him dead in his chair with several empty brandy bottles beside him. Seeking Lethe, perhaps. He'd been reading Hesiod's *Theogony*."

Brandon sat in the leather armchair opposite. "We don't always know what demons a man must deal with."

"He never got over my mother and brother's death. Bart was his favorite son, and as his heir, he always spent more time with him. Riding about the estate. He took great interest in it in those days."

"Still, you were his heir. He should have done the same for you."

"But he never did. That can't have been a comfortable thing for him to take with him to Hades."

"No, indeed."

"I was at fault, too, I suppose. Once I joined the army, I didn't see much of him. I feel some pity for him now." Reade shrugged off the melancholy that had settled over him and grinned at his friend. "Let's choose a more attractive topic of conversation. I spied the most delightful young woman as I entered the city this afternoon."

"Oh? A shop girl or a prostitute on a street corner?"

"*Au contraire.* This girl wore gloves and a fetching bonnet. She was traveling in a deplorable vehicle with her family. A fresh-faced angel, Cartwright, with a mouth to make a man dream."

Brandon chuckled. "Good to see you're regaining your equilibrium."

CHAPTER TWO

J O'S FIRST BALL was held the following Saturday, and to distract herself from the butterflies in her stomach, she thought about Mrs. Millet. How had she arranged the invitations so quickly? Wouldn't they have to be sent weeks prior to the event? The fluttering increased, and she felt slightly sick.

The dressmaker in Piccadilly Mrs. Millet recommended, fitted Jo for several outfits. Madame Moreau ran a large establishment and knew her business, but Jo found her as snooty as their butler and not nearly as endearing as Mrs. Laverty in Marlborough. As no dresses would be ready until the following week, Jo was thankful to have the ballgown Mrs. Laverty had made for her.

They'd had little chance to see London. She and Aunt Mary made some hurried purchases in the shops near the dressmaker's rooms. Jo purchased a blue satin hat with a soft white feather, and a painted fan made of ivory sticks with a silk tassel. She chose a silk shawl as a gift for Mrs. Laverty.

The shop fronts displayed exotic wares. It was noisy and exciting, with bustling pedestrians, the shoppers strolling the pavements while vehicles crammed the roads. She could have stayed for hours looking into shop windows, but Aunt Mary complained of sore feet, so Jo hailed a hackney, and they went home.

On the evening of the ball, Sally helped Jo dress and arranged her hair as best she could. Disappointed, Jo stood before the Cheval mirror to study the effect. The color of the ballgown suited her, but the fussy style didn't. Even her mother's pearl necklace failed to improve it.

"It makes me look a bit...lumpy," Jo said in despair.

"I think it's pretty, Miss Jo." Sally was fresh from the country with no more idea of the ways of Society than Jo, but she was eager to learn and friendly, which Jo appreciated.

Jo gave the blonde maid an encouraging smile. "We shall learn together, Sally." She shrugged. "I'm afraid I have no recourse but to wear it." She gathered up her shawl, reticule, and fan and went down to join her father, determined to enjoy her first ball even if she sat out every dance for the entire evening.

Her father smiled as she entered the parlor. "You look beautiful, Jo."

Aunt Mary, beside him in purple and black lace, warmly agreed.

Mrs. Millet was there to greet them in the hall of the Rivenstock's townhouse in Westminster. She introduced them to their host and hostess. Lord Rivenstock, his crimson waistcoat straining over an enormous stomach, rudely viewed Jo from head to toe through his quizzing glass on its black velvet ribbon. His wife merely nodded before turning to welcome the other guests. Jo's face felt stiff, and her smile wavered.

They entered the ballroom, gaily festooned with lanterns, and decorated with vases of flowers on every table. Jo wondered again why the Rivenstocks had issued them an invitation. Were they paid? Or might they owe Mrs. Millet a favor?

Jo refused to let such concerns spoil her first ball, her attention captured by the smoky ballroom crammed with noisy guests dressed in glorious finery. A footman took them to their chairs, and a handsome young footman approached with a tray of champagne and lemonade. When Jo's hand hovered over the glass, the footman cleared his throat.

She glanced up at him, then remembered Mrs. Millet's advice. Young ladies did not drink champagne. The footman angled the tray to bring the lemonade closer. Jo gave him a smile and took it, and was glad of it, for the ballroom, a series of rooms opened to form one long space, was stuffy and overheated. The overly perfumed guests mingled on the edge of the dance floor and barely glanced their way. They might have been part of the wallpaper, which was a bilious green decorated with gold ribbons and bows.

An hour passed, and another set ended. The young footman reappeared. He raised his eyebrows when she took a glass of champagne. He smiled at Jo's shrug and moved away. Jo had a glass of Madeira once and hadn't much cared for it, but the champagne was infinitely better. After she'd finished the glass, her nervousness eased.

At the announcement of a quadrille, people left their seats and crossed the floor with their partners. Her father had engaged a Frenchman, Monsieur Forage, to teach Jo the dance steps. While she had danced at assemblies, her partners could not be compared to the elegant gentlemen here.

When the orchestra on the dais struck up, she tried not to wriggle her toes, longing to join the dancers on the floor. But no gentleman asked her. Growing despondent, Jo watched the dancers going through the steps. The young ladies were in white or the palest pastels. Aware of how wrong she looked, Jo sat, her back as stiff as a poker, while Aunt Mary talked with Mrs. Millet.

Her father had become friendly with a couple who hailed from Wiltshire. He regaled them with how Jo had been delightfully plump and freckled as a child and excelled at the lute. "She has her mother's gift, she sings like an angel," she heard him say. Jo cringed and wanted to cover her ears. Hot with embarrassment, she swished her fan before her face, praying for a gentleman to rescue her.

No one did. She sat, her chest tight with distress, watching the dance until its conclusion, and then the couples promenading from the floor.

Two debutantes sashayed past Jo. They glanced at her and giggled behind their fans. Their dresses of white muslin embroidered with tiny flowers and trimmed with ribbons, were exactly like the illustration Jo found. Jo wistfully admired them. They were like dainty blossoms, from their elegant heads to their satin slippers.

She placed a hand over the saucer-shaped green silk camellia above her navel. She dropped her gaze, unsure where to look, fearing everyone in the ballroom laughed at her. How totally lacking in style, she was. How could she be so gauche? So foolish?

She sat out the country dance, which seemed interminable. During the break, two women walked past her, casting her curious glances.

"Who is she?" the lady in puce asked the woman beside her.

"No idea. They come from far and wide to the Rivenstocks' balls and pay for the privilege," the other lady said.

So, it was true! Mrs. Millet had paid the Rivenstocks to invite them!

As the women strolled away, Jo heard the lady in puce ask her friend, "Where on earth did she get that dress?" Jo sat rigid in her seat, fearing her father overheard. Fortunately, he was now talking about his shop.

When she couldn't bear it another minute, Jo excused herself and went in search of the ladies' retiring room. She hurried inside, relieved to find no attendant and no one behind the screen provided for a lady's modesty.

Jo flopped down onto the settee, but a moment later, the door opened, and a young lady in rose-pink brocade entered, her dark brown hair styled elegantly to display a long, graceful neck. Diamonds sparkled in her ears and adorned her throat and wrist.

Crushed, Jo rose to tidy herself before the mirror. She frowned at her image. Her heavy dark red locks defied any attempt to tame them and were escaping the pins, the arrangement in imminent danger of collapse.

The lady smiled at Jo's reflection. "Your first ball?"

Jo sighed. "Is it so obvious?"

Her smile widened. "Mrs. Letitia Cartwright. How do you do?"

"Miss Joanna Dalrymple, and not very well, I'm afraid. My hair is beyond help, and I hate my dress. I should ask my father to take me home." She gathered up her shawl and reticule from a chair and turned to leave the room.

Letitia put a hand on her arm. "Please stay a moment. Might we talk? I gather you are new to London?"

Jo feared another snub. "Yes, we arrived a week ago from Wiltshire."

"It takes a while to accustom oneself to how we do things here. It's all a mystery at first, especially the rules and dictums of Society. I found it challenging myself at first."

Jo raised her eyebrows. "You did?" She could not believe this elegant lady could suffer such humiliation.

"I came from Cumbria. My first Season in London was awkward and then...well, most unusual. But that's a story for another time."

Letitia didn't seem much older than Jo herself. "Did you meet your husband during the Season?"

Laughter warmed her brown eyes. "I did, yes."

"I shan't be so fortunate. Not tonight, at least." Jo pulled a face and turned away from her image. "My dress is all wrong, Mrs. Cartwright."

"Please call me Letty."

"Letty. I'm Jo," she said shyly.

"I had a similar experience, Jo. In fact, it was that which drew me to you."

"Oh?" Jo studied Letty's beautiful ballgown in disbelief.

"My aunt had antiquated ideas about dress. You are far more fortunate than I was. My gown featured a large double ruffle around the neck, which one might find on a lizard."

"Oh, no!" Jo giggled.

Letty grinned. "The style of your gown is fashionable, but the flowers detract from the overall picture, don't you think?"

"I wanted rosebuds," Jo admitted.

She nodded sympathetically. "Let me see what I can do." She studied the gown, from the largest flower on the skirt to the smallest decorating the short sleeves, and those rioting around the bottom.

Her face burning, Jo stood in silence while Letty considered it. How mortifying. She would love to go home, but how could she disappoint her father and Aunt Mary? It was insupportable.

"We can improve it," Letty said finally.

"How?" Jo couldn't help being hopeful. Letty seemed confident.

"With these." Letty opened her reticule and took out a pair of scissors. "Let's remove some of those flowers."

"Oh... do you think we should?" Jo's eyes widened in the mirror. What if Letty cut a hole in her dress?

"I do." Letty took hold of the flower positioned near Jo's navel and cut the threads holding it in place. The camellia came away in her hand.

Jo turned to the mirror. Her gown was better without it.

She tried not to tremble as Letty snipped away. More flowers fell to the floor. She kneeled to remove some of those crowding the hem, then straightened and made Jo turn around. "I like the sleeves, they're pretty, we shall leave them," Letty decided as she viewed her handiwork. "The gown is quite elegant now, don't you think so?"

"Yes. I do," Jo said cautiously, moving closer to the mirror. There were no holes in the fabric, and the change was miraculous.

"Now, please sit. The style of your hair is too severe."

Letty fashioned a knot high on Jo's head, then teased a few long curls to rest against her neck and face. Taking a hairpin from her reticule, she tucked one of the smaller camellias into Jo's hair behind her ear. "You have beautiful hair."

"There's too much of it. It's difficult to manage," Jo admitted.

"Every woman should have such a problem." Letty laughed. "It is your crowning glory, Jo."

"That is what my father says," she admitted.

"He is quite right. A good cut will make it more manageable. I can recommend my hairdresser. I'll give you her address if you wish to use her."

"I would appreciate it, thank you, Letty."

Letty smiled. "Now, give me your opinion. Have I wrought magic?"

Jo rose to study herself in the mirror. Her gown was still unlike the other debutantes', but it looked much better. Even the small flowers decorating the sleeves looked pretty. Jo turned a shoulder to better view her hair. She approved of the camellia.

Jo twirled. "I love it." She grinned. "I can't thank you enough, Letty."

"I should like us to talk again," Letty said. "But Cartwright and I always dance the waltz. The *ton* frown on a woman dancing with her husband, but I suspect they have grown used to us."

The waltz was called as she and Letty returned to the ballroom. Letty said goodbye and joined a tall, dark-haired man who led her onto the dance floor. Mr. Cartwright was handsome. He smiled down at his wife with such affection, it sent a flood of longing through Jo's chest. Would a man *ever* look at her that way?

Aunt Mary gasped when Jo returned to her chair. "What have you done to your beautiful gown?"

"Improved on it," Jo said with an impish grin.

"Well, we mustn't tell Mrs. Laverty," her aunt said, after considering it. "But, I must admit the simpler style flatters you."

Jo took a seat beside her aunt. She raised her chin at an appraising glance from a young debutante who had rudely stared at her earlier. "I shall tell Mrs. Laverty that I wore her gown and had a wonderful time at my first ball."

Aunt Mary nodded in approval. "You are always kind-hearted, Jo."

But at her next ball, Jo would wear the white muslin she'd requested from her new dressmaker.

Mrs. Millet introduced them to Mr. Baxter, a thin gentleman with gray streaks in his hair. He promptly asked her to dance the Roger de Coverley.

Jo rested her fingers on his arm while offering silent thanks to Letty. Mr. Baxter was too old for her to consider a suitor, but she was to dance, and as they joined the other dancers on the floor, decided the evening had taken a turn for the better.

As Mr. Baxter returned Jo to her chair, she saw a dark-haired gentleman with Letty and Mr. Cartwright. It was the man from the black coach who greeted her when they first entered the city. He and the Cartwrights seemed on good terms as they laughed together. Taller than Mr. Cartwright, with an athletic physique, he stood as if confident in his own skin. She struggled not to glance his way too often, curious to know if he recognized her. But he showed no sign of it.

Jo danced twice more with two different gentlemen. Mr. Baxter took her in to supper. He was a pleasant man, but he spoke almost exclusively about his young baby and recently deceased wife and seemed very sad. The ball ended in the early hours. Exhausted, her eyelids heavy, she climbed into their hired carriage, with her body still thrumming with excitement. The rest of the Season awaited them, and her lovely new wardrobe of gowns.

"Did you enjoy your first ball, Jo?" her father asked as they passed through shadowy streets, which appeared magical, lit by the gas lamps. "Yes, Papa. It was exciting." Although no man she danced with interested her, and one had made disparaging remarks about her being a country lass.

Jo knew exactly what she wanted in a husband. He would be attractive, rather like the gentleman in the black coach, but more importantly, a caring companion with whom she could share life's joys and toils.

"Mrs. Millet proves to be a remarkably efficient woman. She has been spreading the news of your handsome dowry," Papa said. "But I shall assess any gentleman carefully." He smiled at her. "It will be a very special man who deserves my daughter."

"Oh, Papa." Jo smiled and leaned against his shoulder, which smelled of pipe smoke. It was all very well to dream, but the thought of an actual flesh and blood suitor caused her stomach to flip. "I hope I don't disappoint you."

"As if you could." Her father placed an arm around her. "It was fortunate that Mrs. Millet not only recommended the dressmaker but forwarded your measurements to her on our behalf. Such a helpful lady." Her father's voice had grown warm. Jo glanced up at him, but in the dim interior of the carriage, she could not make out his expression. Was he growing fond of Mrs. Millet? Jo wasn't sure what she thought of that.

"I met the nicest lady tonight," she said, yawning behind her gloved hand. "Mrs. Letitia Cartwright. Letty was very helpful." Her father had not noticed the changes to her dress.

"Making friends already. That's my girl," Papa said with a fond chuckle.

And there was a handsome gentleman with hair as black as coal, Jo thought sleepily. However, she didn't say it aloud.

EARLIER, READE HAD watched Letty talking to the red-haired angel he'd seen a few days prior on his way into London.

"You appear acquainted with the lady in green," Reade said when

Letty joined him and Cartwright.

Letty narrowed her eyes at him, a smile curling her lips. "Only in passing. Not well enough to introduce you."

"Your wife does not wish me to meet the lady," Reade complained to her husband.

Brandon shrugged. "She considers you too disreputable, Reade."

Reade laughed. "And so, I am. But what of it? Surely a dance with the pretty redhead is harmless enough?"

"Nothing about you is harmless, Reade," Letty said, a smile teasing her lips. "You are so often in my husband's company, I believe I have your measure."

"Ho," Reade said, enjoying himself. "I am merely putty in a lady's hands."

The laughter faded in Letty's eyes. "Miss Dalrymple is fresh from the country and has yet to learn Society's ways. I beg that you will be kind."

He took umbrage at that. "I am never unkind to a lady."

"But we are discussing innocent young maidens. They come to London to find a husband, not to have their heads turned by a…a…" She paused as Brandon's murmured disapproval censured her.

"A rake?" Reade filled in the word for her. He frowned. "I am intensely unhappy you think me thus."

Letty took his arm. "I do not think you a rake, Reade. I merely consider you unsuitable."

"As indeed, I am. And while I bow to your better judgment in this matter, one dance will not compromise the young lady. If you'll kindly introduce me." Reade turned to where the young woman in green had been sitting. It appeared she and her family had left the ballroom. "Ah, I fear she has retired. Next time?"

Letty relented with a sigh. "If you wish. But you will unsettle her."

He raised an eyebrow. "How should I?"

"She will unfairly compare you to the other gentleman seeking a bride this Season," she said.

"And an insipid lot most of them are," Brandon said as he placed his champagne glass on a footman's tray.

"I am overwhelmed," Reade said with a chuckle.

"It is something you and Cartwright both have. An aura. You fascinate women."

"She is very loyal, my bride," Cartwright said with a laugh. "Shall we concentrate on the reason we are here at this appalling affair?" he asked Reade.

"I thought as much." Letty raised her eyebrows. "What *is* the reason we have come to this ball? I detest our host."

"Nothing to concern yourself with, my love." Brandon bowed. "If you will excuse us."

Letty gave a slight bob. "I shall, my lord, as we can talk later."

Her husband cocked a brow. "I might not have talk in mind, later, my love."

"But I do," Letty said with a sweet smile.

Reade chuckled. "I don't know how you manage this all too clever wife of yours, Cartwright."

"It takes some astute maneuvering," Brandon said with a grin.

"It works well." Letty gathered up her shawl, reticule, and fan. "Because I allow Brandon to believe it. Ah, there is Lady Sommerville, I promised to give her a recipe for gooseberry cheese."

"Minx," Brandon murmured, looking appreciative. Once his wife moved out of earshot, he turned to Reade and placed a hand on his shoulder. "I daresay Viscount Sidmouth is waiting."

"I'm curious as to why the Home Office has involved us in a matter ordinarily left to Bow Street," Reade said as they crossed the floor. "Has Sidmouth some interest in tonight's host?"

"A bigger fish, methinks. But you may make a variety of guesses," Brandon said as they walked to the library. "It's my hope he is about to tell us, and quickly, so I might remove my lady to home and bed."

Reade chuckled. He would not be averse to marriage if he could find a lady like Letitia Cartwright. Dashed if he wouldn't. But then, that would mean upending a way of life that served him well. And what could he offer a wife? A drafty estate in the north, filled with such painful memories that he hardly ever visited? He would not fool himself into believing he could make a woman happy. It would not be fair to the lady.

The library was empty. "It appears Sidmouth has got caught up somewhere," Brandon said resignedly.

Reade stretched his length out from a padded chair and watched the flames lick into the wood. "Nice of them to light us a fire, though, pass the brandy decanter, there's a good fellow."

CHAPTER THREE

T HE NEXT MORNING, the two gentlemen who partnered Jo at the ball, and Mr. Baxter sent their cards. They called promptly at two o'clock in the afternoon. Mr. Baxter silently drank his tea while he eyed the other gentlemen with an expression of grave censure. Although Jo would never consider Mr. Baxter for a husband, she agreed with him. She distrusted the way the other two fawned on her. They effusively agreed with everything she said as if she was an oracle or a renowned beauty.

"Well, you are beautiful, Jo," her father said when she moaned to him later. "But I believe they have learned of our improved financial circumstances."

She disliked being judged by her father's wealth and the size of her dowry. To suddenly become a person of consequence sat awkwardly on her shoulders. If it meant people treated her differently, she wouldn't care for it. Back in Wiltshire, she was on good terms with everyone, except those up at the manor, to whom she remained virtually invisible.

"It is the way of the world, Jo," her father said.

"Well, I don't care for it."

"Nor I. Even though my circumstances have changed, I will never judge a man by his fortune," he said. "Unlike your mother's family, who cast your mother and your aunt out because of me."

It always made Jo mad. Her father was the best of fellows.

The order at Madame Moreau's salon was all but finished. The dressmaker was as English as Jo was, for her French accent slipped on occasion to become something less refined, but Madame knew what clothes a debutante needed, and Jo's confidence in her grew. A room full of needlewomen finished several outfits to a very high standard. A cape of gold cloth trimmed with soft sable, an elegant green and white satin carriage dress, and a striped sarsenet promenade dress with Vandyke edging. The white silk evening gown decorated with gold braid made Jo catch her breath. She would purchase gold slippers to wear with it.

Madame's recommendations sent Jo and Aunt Mary to the best establishments to purchase hats and accessories. Jo bought a fetching leghorn bonnet ornamented with a plume of down feathers and another bonnet of white velvet trimmed with satin, several pairs of white gloves, and a pair of primrose leather, and a frilly white parasol. Aunt Mary chose a lovely India shawl, a white crepe fan embroidered with silver, and a lace cap with a broad satin bow.

At five o'clock the following day, she and her aunt promenaded in Hyde Park among the fashionable ladies and gentlemen. Jo watched the riders trot down Rotten Row while searching fruitlessly for a large dark-haired gentleman.

That evening they listened to the wail of bagpipes in Astley's Amphitheater and watched tumblers, clowns, and bareback riders stand atop galloping horses in an awe-inspiring display. A loud collective gasp rose from the crowd as a rider dived through a ring of fire and landed back on the horse. Aunt Mary squealed and put her hands to her face when a tight-rope walker high on a rope above the ring appeared about to tumble to his death but caught the rope just in time. It was all part of the act. Silence fell as a beautiful white horse danced to a tune played by a fiddler. And then it was over.

As they left in the crowd, Aunt Mary grabbed Jo's arm. "I believe I saw Mrs. Millet."

"Mrs. Millet is here?" Her father turned to look. "Where?"

Aunt Mary searched the jostling crowd. "I cannot find her now. Perhaps I was mistaken."

"I'm sure you were, Mary," he said. "I told Mrs. Millet of our plans. She would join us, I'm sure."

"It is Mrs. Millet," Jo said. She departed the arena with a tall, thin man with white hair. He glanced over his shoulder, and for a moment, his gray eyes met Jo's. She shivered. They were the coldest eyes she had ever seen.

"I suppose she couldn't find us in this crowd," her father said.

Jo smiled and took his arm, but it left her perturbed.

As the days passed, Jo gained confidence in finding her way around Mayfair and its environs with Sally, and they returned to the dressmaker's rooms again. Jo's ballgown was not the muslin she'd hoped for, but a beautiful pale blue sarsnet, worn over a white satin slip, cut low, with a sash of satin riband, fastened in a bow in front and ornamented with a deep trimming of net. It was quite the loveliest dress she'd ever seen. The rest of her wardrobe would be delivered later in the afternoon. After a last fitting, Jo had her hair cut by the hairdresser Letty recommended.

The woman set about the task, comb and scissors poised, while Jo sat nervously in the chair. Inches were lopped off and fell in piles on the floor. When she finished, Jo, unsure, glanced this way and that in the mirror. She felt light-headed as she came home with Sally. Calling for the tea tray and a special request for scones, she sank into a chair in the parlor.

A kitchen maid brought in the tea tray. She unstacked the tea things onto the table. "Oh, you've had your hair cut, Miss Dalrymple. It's ever so smart with those shorter bits in front."

Relieved, Jo smiled at the maid. Not that she was particularly vain about her hair, she just wanted to look right. "Thank you, Milly." She was on good terms with all the servants, except the butler, who maintained his snobbish demeanor. "Mm, scones and lemon tarts, my favorites, please thank Cook."

"I will, miss." Milly bobbed and left the room.

Pleased with her day, Jo poured the tea from the rose painted teapot into porcelain cups for herself and her father, who had just wandered in. Aunt Mary had declared herself weary and asked to have a tray sent to her room.

She drank her tea, then left her father puffing on his pipe and reading the broadsheets to go to her bedchamber. Sally hovered over a pile of boxes and brown-paper packages. Her blue eyes danced, a pair of scissors already poised in her hand. "Ooh, Miss Jo, shall I cut the string?"

Jo hurried over to the bed. "Please do, Sally."

Soon, the empty boxes sat discarded on the floor along with piles of tissue paper. The ball gown was perfect. She would look just the thing when at her next ball.

They received another invitation to a ball close by in Mayfair. Her father told her that Mrs. Millet was working tirelessly on their behalf. He had learned she'd fallen on hard times since Mr. Millet died.

Sally, who was quickly learning her role of lady's maid, curled Jo's hair in papers. The evening of the ball, Jo sat before the mirror in her chemise and petticoats while Sally coaxed her curls into a modern style, lower on the forehead and partly braided with a half-wreath of spring flowers. A light application of powder and Jo slipped into the ballgown. She wore her mother's pearl earrings and the gold heart-shaped locket her father had given her for her birthday. With the addition of a pretty shawl, shoes of white satin, and white gloves above the elbow, Jo was ready.

Unlike the Rivenstocks, Lady Montford proved to be a charming hostess. Pleased with her appearance, Jo was determined to enjoy herself. Either Mrs. Millet had done as she promised and zealously spread the news of Jo's handsome dowry, or it was her beautiful ballgown that brought men to her to request an introduction.

Jo danced every dance. The ball was similar to the last, differing only in its superior décor. There were familiar faces among the guests and the evening progressed very much like the last.

Jo sat between dances, sipping lemonade when a girl in white muslin approached her with a friendly smile. She was unusually tall and slender, the feathers in the headdress adorning her fair hair stressing her height.

"Charlotte Graham, how do you do? I noticed you sitting alone, and as I have no one to talk to, I wondered if I might join you."

Jo gestured to the seat beside her. "Please do, Miss Graham. Joanna Dalrymple."

Charlotte took the spare seat beside Jo. "Call me Charlotte. Is this your first time in London? I haven't seen you before. I'm sure I'd remember if I had."

"Call me, Jo, please. I am new to London. Are you?"

"Good heavens, no. This is my third Season."

"Oh." Jo didn't know quite what to say to that. She never imagined some girls would come Season after Season without finding a husband.

"It happens. I haven't taken." Charlotte smiled good-naturedly. "My grandfather insists I come every year, even though he's of the opinion that I'm too tall to attract a husband. My dowry isn't particularly large, either."

"Do you enjoy coming to London?"

"I don't mind. Our small Devonshire village is rather dull. The worst thing is I make friends among the debutantes but see little of them after they marry." She eyed Jo appreciatively. "You won't be sitting here like a wallflower for long. A gentleman will snap you up."

"A wallflower?"

"That's what we call ourselves." Charlotte shrugged. "I made a good friend last Season. Miss Anabel Riley. But she disappeared from

London."

"Did she get married?"

Charlotte shrugged. "No one seems to know what happened to Anabel. She was an orphan, here with an aged aunt who has since died. Some say she eloped, but I don't believe it. Anabel never mentioned a beau."

Charlotte stood as the Master of Ceremonies announced the next dance. "I'd best return to Mrs. Lincoln. That's my chaperone. I've enjoyed talking with you."

Jo smiled. "I hope we meet again."

"We will," Charlotte said. "I'll look out for you."

Charlotte's feather headdress could be seen above many heads as she moved through the crowd. Jo hoped they could be friends. A gentleman came to claim the dance she had agreed to earlier. As he led her onto the dance floor, she wondered what had happened to Anabel Riley. Perhaps her family came and took her away. But no, Charlotte had said she was an orphan.

Jo enjoyed the evening but didn't go into raptures about the ball when her father questioned her on their way home. The dark-haired gentleman friend of the Cartwrights had not appeared. She wondered if she would ever see him again. Surely it shouldn't matter whether or not she did. But it seemed to matter a great deal.

Her father declared the Season to be a splendid success. "As I knew it would be." He gazed fondly at her.

"Did you especially like any of the gentlemen, Jo?" Aunt Mary asked.

"Not really, Aunt." Jo supposed she was used to country folk, who were plain speaking.

Some of her dance partners used an oddly affected manner of speech. One gentleman had ridiculously padded shoulders, and another older one creaked mysteriously as he led her through the steps of the quadrille, and was so heavily perfumed, she wished to hold her nose. Some of her dance partners barely spoke, so Jo was hard-pressed to think of an appropriate topic of conversation, while others talked about themselves, their last successful hunt, the acquisition of a curricle, one gentleman went into raptures about his tailor. None showed any genuine interest in her. "I made another friend, Miss Charlotte Graham, Papa. I hope to meet her again."

"I'm so pleased for you, Jo," Aunt Mary said, wearily.

"That's nice, Jo," her father said. "I hoped you might meet some fellow...well...it's early days."

Might he want to go home? He expressed some concern about Sooty, although their dog was enjoying a holiday on a farm. Perhaps London wasn't her father's cup of tea.

As she drank her chocolate in bed the following morning, Jo went over the previous evening. She had difficulty bringing her dance partners to mind, except for Mr. Luttrell. And she only remembered him because he'd taken her into supper. His interest was horses. While he talked about the finer points of the thoroughbred he'd purchased at Tattersall's horse auction, Jo fixed an interested expression on her face and allowed her gaze to wander, seeking a tall, dark-haired gentleman.

She sighed and put down her cup. Licking the chocolate from her upper lip, she admitted she'd spent the entire evening on the lookout for him. But neither he nor the Cartwrights attended the ball.

THERE WERE FEW clouds to shadow the moon, for which Reade was grateful. He found his way with ease across the lawns without stumbling over the many flowerpots the lady of the house seemed overly fond of and reached the brick wall at the rear of the house. Most of the building lay in darkness, but for a lamp in the front hall and a glimmer from a sconce on the upstairs landing.

He circled the house, moving through the shadows. The two occupants were out for the evening. The servants had retired to their attic rooms, except for one who awaited his employer's return. Reade tried several windows and found them locked. He couldn't risk jimmying a window open. On closer inspection, a casement window on the second floor was ajar, but there were no trees nearby to aid his climb.

It would have to be the drainpipe. He prayed it would bear his weight. When Reade took hold and shinnied up, the pipe shifted alarmingly beneath his hands and threatened to come away from the wall. But his luck was in, for it held, and he reached the next floor without mishap. His searching fingers located a crevice in the bricks. He swung himself across to the window and levered himself up onto the sill. Swinging his legs over, he dropped soundlessly onto the carpet.

Moonlight flooded in, revealing the room to be a bedchamber as he'd expected, and of no use to him. He stalked soft-footed to the door and listened. No snoring reached him, only the clunk of a clock and the scrabble of mice in the walls. He knew the residents were at a ball and unlikely to return until close to dawn. That should give him a few hours to inspect the library at his leisure.

On the landing, a guttering candle flickered in a sconce, lighting the stairs. Descending, he grimaced at the sharp creaks of the treads beneath his boots. One of the annoying things about being large. Reade was a heavyweight and always had to make allowances for it. He could handle himself well in a skirmish, but smaller men in the game had the advantage in matters of stealth.

When he reached the bottom of the stairs, loud snores greeted him from the servant slumbering on a chair near the front door. Having some knowledge of the layout of the house from previous visits, Reade located the library without mishap. He entered and quietly closed the door, then went straight to the desk set against the far wall. Moonlight shone in through the break in the velvet curtains and revealed a stack of papers scattered over the oak surface, but not bright enough for him to read them. It forced him to pull the curtains shut and strike a taper. A dangerous move, but necessary.

The feeble light enabled him to scan them. He had splendid night vision. Two letters were immediately of interest. A delivery notice and a letter detailing the date of a meeting somewhere near the docks, but not the exact address. He slid both into his coat pocket, where his pistol rested, then turned his attention to the others.

A ruckus outside drew him to the window. A lumbering carriage with swinging lamps passed through the gates and rattled along the drive to the stables. Reade snuffed the taper between his fingers. Home early, curse it.

The snores in the hall ended with a curse and a scrape of a chair as Reade slipped back into the corridor. He made for the servants' stairs, planning to leave through the kitchen.

Twenty minutes later, he crouched in the bushes to watch the house. The man and woman climbed the staircase; candlelight showed their progress in the long window. He considered going back inside after they fell asleep, but abandoned the idea as unsound and turned away. There was always another night, and what he had in his pocket might well prove interesting enough. He'd let those at the Home Office make a judgment and await further orders.

Once well clear of the house, Reade vaulted a fence and sprinted down the lane to where he'd left his horse tied to a post. He released the reins and mounted. "Enough for one evening, eh, Ash?" he murmured. "You'll be wanting your dry, warm stall, and I'm tempted to don evening togs and attend a ball to flirt with the ladies." He thought briefly of the redhead, but in full agreement with Letty's advice, dismissed any idea of pursuit. "Methinks, I'll go to bed." He patted the gelding's glossy neck and trotted him quietly down the road by the light of a sickle moon.

CHAPTER FOUR

AN INVITATION TO a masked ball arrived in the post. The demands of the Season surprised Jo. One might dine with friends, then go to the theater or a soiree, before attending a ball, all on the same evening. Guests roamed from one reception to the next. Apparently, hostesses attempted to outdo one another, perhaps to gain some distinction on the social calendar, sometimes adopting what Jo considered outlandish displays.

Why the *ton* weren't all thoroughly exhausted mystified her until she learned that many slept past midday. Jo was wide awake by seven o'clock, no matter what time she climbed into bed. Her Aunt Mary fussed over her and insisted Jo take an afternoon nap when she retired for hers. Used to filling her days productively, Jo lay reading in bed until her father allowed her to get up again.

The evening of the masked ball, they were greeted by the Viscount and Viscountess Lisle and entered the festooned ballroom. Her father excused himself to search for the mask he'd dropped on the way in from the carriage. The last strains of music died away as a country dance ended. From their seats, Jo and Aunt Mary watched the dancers leave the floor, laughing and cavorting and enjoying the freedom of their disguises.

When Aunt Mary complained of the discomfort of peering through slits and fiddled with the ties on her pink mask, Jo realized that it prevented her from wearing her glasses. A half-hour passed, while they wondered where her father had got to.

Mrs. Millet approached them with a slim, fair-haired gentleman at her side. He was of average height and wore a black mask, his crimson cape pushed back over his shoulders.

"Miss Hatton, Miss Dalrymple, I should like to introduce you to Mr. Ollerton."

"Ah, you have given me away, Madam. Were we not to be unmasked at midnight?" Mr. Ollerton smiled, revealing even, white teeth. The candlelight from the enormous chandelier overhead painted his hair gold.

"Forgive me, Mr. Ollerton," Mrs. Millet tittered. "I could not introduce you to these ladies otherwise. And you did insist."

Jo wondered why he wished so ardently to meet her when her mask hid most of her face. But she smiled to welcome him.

He sat for a moment and chatted with Aunt Mary, who was effusively describing her new cottage garden and her cats.

A good listener, Mr. Ollerton seemed kind-hearted.

The waltz was announced, and the musicians tuned their instruments. "Would you give me the pleasure of this dance, Miss Dalrymple?"

Jumping up, Jo bobbed. "Delighted, sir."

"Jo, I'm not sure you should…" Aunt Mary began.

"No such rule applies at a masked ball," Mrs. Millet said firmly. She had instructed Jo earlier to only waltz with her father. Jo thought it a silly convention.

The dance seemed perfectly respectable, although perhaps more license might be taken. But she wasn't about to bring it into question, for she longed to waltz. With a smile, she rested her fingers on the gentleman's arm, and he led her onto the dance floor.

Mr. Ollerton danced well. At first, surprised by their closeness, she was enjoying her first waltz, when he spoke and drew her attention to what she could see of him below the mask, his mouth and rounded chin shaved smooth.

"You hail from the country, Miss Dalrymple?" He led her through a turn. "Near Bath, I believe?"

"Marlborough, sir."

Jo waited for him to lose interest as another gentleman had done.

"Beautiful countryside in those parts. I know of the Marlborough white horse," he said. "I went to view the figure on the hill when traveling once to Bath. It stands out impressively. However, I am not cognizant of its history."

"A boy named William Canning designed the figure of the horse and marked it out early this century with the help of the other boys from Mr. Greasley's Academy," Jo said. "William's family owned the Manor House at Osbourne St. George."

"Fascinating," he said with his attractive smile. "Will you promise to tell me more? If I may call on you tomorrow?"

"I should be happy to," Jo said, pleased for the chance to see him again.

He exhibited a pleasing lack of condescension. While she would have to see more of him to judge, he could fit her idea of a husband. He was one of the most interesting men she had met. And the most elegant. The cut of his coat spoke of fine tailoring, his cravat tied in an intricate knot, and a fine gold fob decorated his white silk waistcoat. Perhaps he was wealthy and had no interest in her dowry. She caught her lip in her teeth in consternation. When had she become so hard-hearted and suspicious? And she was yet to see his face. What color were his eyes? Impossible to tell through the slits of his mask. Hazel, perhaps.

"An elegant gentleman with exquisite manners," Aunt Mary said approvingly when he had left them.

"Yes." Jo watched him make his way through the crowd. "He is to call on us tomorrow."

"My, my," her aunt said. She fell silent, offering no further opinion.

"Then you approve of me waltzing with him, Aunt?" Jo asked after a moment. Her aunt was usually forthcoming in her opinions.

"I like to see you enjoying yourself. They didn't dance the waltz in ballrooms in my day. I have to admit it looks exhilarating." She waved her fan before her face. "As long as you don't come under criticism."

"I doubt I'm of any interest," Jo said. No one paid the slightest attention to her.

"But you are. You're the prettiest debutante here tonight."

Jo smiled at her loyal aunt. "I'm not, but thank you for saying so."

Why had her aunt never married? Her father told Jo she had settled into spinsterhood at a young age. Was it because she was nearsighted and forced to wear glasses? Had it made her shy? Aunt Mary's support for Jo's mother and father had enraged their brother, Sir Brian Endicott. He and Lady Endicott ostracized her mother and sent Aunt Mary packing, too. With nowhere to go, Jo's parents took her aunt in. She seemed content not to marry, but to Jo, it seemed a poor life compared to the love of a husband and children.

At midnight they announced the unmasking. Laughter rippled through the room as masks came off. Relieved to remove hers, Jo searched for Mr. Ollerton but could find no sign of him. Had he left the ball? Perhaps he wasn't interested in her. Disappointed, she danced another set, while her father, his mask pushed up on his forehead, danced with Mrs. Millet. Jo felt torn. While she was pleased for her father, who had remained loyal to her mother's memory too long in her opinion, was, at last, enjoying himself in a lady's company. She wished she could like that lady more.

Letty emerged from the crowd in gold silk, a black lace mask trailing from her fingers by its strings. Jo heard her infectious laugh as she wandered in their direction. A gentleman walked at her elbow, her husband, Mr. Cartwright. Jo sat forward in her seat when the dark-haired gentleman from the coach, dressed in black and white evening clothes, appeared. He must also have just arrived, she always had an eye out for him, and it would have been impossible not to spot him, for he was head and shoulders above most men here tonight.

With a welcoming smile, Letty approached Jo, accompanied by the two gentlemen. "Miss Dalrymple, and is this Miss Hatton? How good to see you this evening. Allow me to introduce you to my husband, Mr. Cartwright, and our friend, Baron, Lord Reade."

The gentlemen bowed.

Jo took to Mr. Cartwright immediately. His ready smile put her at ease, but when Lord Reade's firm lips curled into a beguiling smile, she felt unusually warm. Up close, he was the perfect depiction of masculine strength and beauty. His large eyes, deep and dark, observed her as if he could easily uncover her secret thoughts. A frisson of awareness rushed through her. She would be totally out of her depth with such a man. Her fingers coiled around her fan while she resisted snapping it open.

A baron, Lord Reade, came from a different world. He would not wish to marry the daughter of a haberdasher. It was just as well, for she couldn't imagine him calling to take tea with her family.

While Letty chattered with her aunt, Lord Reade asked Jo if she approved of masked balls. His voice, low and seductive, held a sardonic note. Did he disapprove of her? Or the ball? A man had come dressed in a harlequin costume and danced around them, making people laugh.

"People's behavior seems to alter while wearing a mask. I saw a gentleman cast himself at a lady's feet and kiss her hem!" Jo said. As she sounded like a prudish governess, she hurried on. "I must admit I like to see people's faces."

"Some faces should never be hidden," the baron said, an appreciative light in his eyes.

Mr. Cartwright chuckled. "And some are the better for the mask."

When Reade's dark eyes remained on her, she lifted her chin.

"What is your opinion of masked balls, my lord?"

"These affairs have distinct advantages, Miss Dalrymple. I might be inclined to cast myself at your feet and kiss your hem."

She gazed into those dark eyes. It was as though he had reached out and touched her. She swallowed. Was he flirting? Or toying with her? "It's not that I'm disapproving of people's actions, sir. I am merely surprised by them."

Reade shrugged wide shoulders. "I am all approval when some of the ridiculous rules set by the doyens of Society are ignored."

"For instance?" Mr. Cartwright prodded with a glimmer of humor in his blue eyes.

Reade shrugged again and cast a lazy smile at his friend. "Has marriage made you forgetful, Cartwright? I shan't remind you of it, however, for it is not suited to a lady's ears."

Cartwright laughed.

"Forgive us, Miss Dalrymple," Lord Reade said. "I should like to hear more of your fresh observations of the *ton*."

"I have none, sir. This is only my third ball."

Dark eyebrows raised over amused eyes. "Then, I must be patient."

He was teasing her! Might it be because she was new to London? A country miss? She had already had experience of such men and felt vaguely disappointed that he was one of them. "That would depend upon whether I'm willing to share them with you, my lord."

Lord Reade bowed gracefully. "*Arrêt à bon temps*," he murmured with that fascinating smile, using a fencing term Jo recognized from a novel.

Mr. Cartwright chuckled. His eyes full of laughter.

Letty paused in her description of the alfresco entertainments found at tea gardens, a mere carriage drive from the city, to raise her eyebrows at them. "I fear I am missing something vastly entertaining."

"We are discussing the merits of masked balls while employing the art of verbal fencing," Mr. Cartwright said. "Miss Dalrymple has made a fine riposte."

Letty smiled and returned to her conversation. The three were obviously on good terms. Jo was pleased with herself for getting the better of him. As he and Cartwright joined into Letty's conversation, she took advantage of the moment to study him. But she had misjudged him; he was not at all condescending. He carried himself like a soldier. Might he have been one? Since the war ended two years ago, many men had sold out.

A second waltz was announced.

"Will you honor me with a dance, Miss Dalrymple?" Lord Reade asked, turning to her.

"Certainly, sir." Surprised that he would ask her, Jo rose and rested her hand on his arm.

Butterflies stirred in her stomach as she walked beside him, aware of the relaxed, effortless power of his movements. Was he a rake? A woman was unlikely to rise disappointed from his bed. The thought was so arousing, heat flooded her face. Jo dropped her chin. Never in her life had she met such a man. A warning voice sounded in her head. *You are out of your depth.*

As they joined those on the dance floor waiting for the waltz to begin, to distract herself from the unsettling presence of the man beside her, she compared him to Mr. Ollerton. They were different in every way imaginable. Reade made little effort to charm her. He was dark, where Ollerton was fair. Reade was no slave to fashion, either. His only adornments were a watch chain and a heavy ornate gold ring on his little finger. His black tailcoat fitted him well across the muscular breadth of his shoulders and required none of the padding some men resorted to. The superfine material was snug at his narrow waist, and his pantaloons emphasized the musculature and length of his legs. While Mr. Ollerton styled his hair in a careful Brutus, Reade's hair was a careless mass of waves which invited one's fingers to order it. Entirely natural, she decided. She smiled at her foolishness. How stupid to form an opinion of a man she'd only just met.

He smiled down at her, his gaze roaming over her face. "Something amuses you?"

"No. It was merely an arbitrary thought."

"Might I be privy to it?"

Caught flat-footed, her chest tightened. *Goodness!* She tried to think of an appropriate answer but failed under his unsettling gaze. "I beg your pardon, my lord. It would not interest you." Her stern tone was meant to put an end to his probing.

That didn't work. A grin imbued his brown eyes with a wicked sparkle. "Then you leave me to speculate, which might be far worse. Come, be honest. I have thick skin."

Really, the man was...impudent. "It is your hair, sir," Jo said, determined to best him.

His eyes widened. "My hair?"

"I approve of the tousled style gentlemen are adopting this Season."

He laughed, causing those dancing nearby to stare. "I merely brush and forget it, Miss Dalrymple. Is that a disappointment to you?"

She demurred. This man would be the undoing of her. She would earn a reputation for being fast and go home in disgrace. And to be fair, she had brought it on herself by agreeing to waltz with him. She should have known better. Where was her head? The few young debutantes on the dance floor would partner their papa or their brother. And she had stood up with a rake. He made her conspicuous, but even so, she admitted that to refuse him would have been impossible.

The music flowed over the ballroom, and he took her in his arms. Her hand clasped firmly in his while the fingers of his other hand spread over her lower back, strong and warm. His touch was like a caress, and his male scent flooded her senses. She couldn't help but to sigh as his body moved with hers over the floor, his long legs brushing her skirts. Being held in his arms appealed to her more than she cared to admit.

He had a commanding self-confidence, which she admired but also distrusted. A man like Reade would not be right for her. She couldn't imagine him in a cozy family setting, chatting to her father over the breakfast table. It was as if danger surrounded him. What an odd thought. How silly she was tonight. Her gaze was drawn again to his face.

Reade lifted his black eyebrows. "Do I pass muster, Miss Dalrymple?"

He was outrageous. When their eyes met, she found it hard to look away. "I could not say, sir," she said, tempted to rebuke him.

He chuckled. "Yet?"

Jo had to laugh. "Do you enjoy teasing me, Lord Reade?"

"I confess I might if it makes your lovely eyes flash daggers at me. But no, Miss Dalrymple. It's just that I prefer to speak my mind. Life is too short for niceties."

"Should we all act like barbarians? Everyone here obeys those rules. Do they not?"

The smile vanished from his eyes. "If you are unaware that some of the gentlemen here tonight with perfect manners are not nearly so polite outside of a ballroom, I should warn you of it."

Jo gazed at him steadily. "Thank you for the warning. But it is entirely unnecessary. I am a fair judge of character." She firmed her lips. She wanted to say she included him in those gentlemen he warned her against, but it would be entirely too impolite.

He swiftly swept her into a series of turns, making her breath catch and her heart hammer. When she could regain her breath, she expected him to continue in the same outrageous vein, as if she were a silly little country miss who must be taught about the big bad city. She was prepared to take him to task, but he smiled. "So, Miss Dalrymple.

What part of England do you hail from?"

She eyed him warily. "Marlborough, my lord."

"I have passed through it, traveling to and from Bath. Never had cause to stop there."

His comment pricked her. "Many do, sir," she said, raising her chin. "Travelers stay at the excellent coaching inn to change carriage horses and tarry awhile." She was about to mention how popular her father's shop had been but resisted the impulse. She would be deeply disappointed if he mocked her.

"I prefer to travel on horseback."

"But you were in a coach when I first saw you." She blushed, realizing she'd given herself away.

"You remember me?" A smile tugged at his lips, and his hand tightened, reminding her of what a strong and vital man he was.

She tried to ignore the thrill prickling her spine. "But of course," she said with false gaiety. "It was my first view of London. I recall every detail of the busy streets, the traffic, and the hawkers. So unlike the country."

"Are you comparing me to a hawker, Miss Dalrymple?"

She laughed. "I was merely describing my first impressions."

"The coach was an unfortunate necessity. I journeyed from the far north. A frustratingly slow way to travel. I don't care to be shut inside a carriage for hours, relying on the expertise of my coachman, although he is a competent fellow. Sometimes I can bear it no longer and climb up on the box to take the reins."

"What took you north, sir?"

"My home lies on the west coast, in Cumbria."

A shadow passed over his features, making her wonder what caused such a sad thought. "And you are pleased to return to London?"

He gazed down at her. "Yes."

She waited, but as he made no further comment, she peeked up at him, taking in the square shape of his jaw. He had an impatient nature, she decided. His character was entirely unfathomable, for he revealed only a glimpse of himself, like ice floating on the Thames. A man with secrets, perhaps. Jo compressed her lips, and he glanced down at her, a query in his eyes.

"I fear you do not approve of me, Miss Dalrymple."

"I don't know you, my lord."

"But you feel that if you did, you would disapprove of me," he said, humor again sparking in his brown eyes.

Jo had to smile. "That is entirely unfair. You are putting words in my mouth."

"And a lovely mouth it is, too." He lowered his glance, making her tremble.

She breathed in deeply. He *was* a rake. And she was quite definitely out of her depth.

It would be far wiser to choose a gentleman like Mr. Ollerton, who was polite and agreeable. There would be no surprises. Reade would never give her a moment's quiet. It was unlikely to be a decision she would ever have to make. And that did not please her as much as it should.

Reade effortlessly turned her again, reminding her of his strength, which she suspected went beyond his well-muscled frame to the core of who he was. Yet, he was mindful in the way he held her and guided their steps while the other dancers swirled around them, the ladies' gowns a blur of color, their voices polite murmurs as they passed, leaving flowery scents in their wake.

Patently aware of his unsettling masculinity, Jo's heart fluttered oddly. What was it about such men women found so intriguing? She had not thought herself one of those women and was a little shame-faced to discover it. There was a commanding air of authority and a hint of steel beneath Mr. Cartwright's exquisite manners, too. Jo felt less chagrinned to realize that Letty also preferred such a man.

She had spied shadows in Reade's dark gaze. If he had been a soldier, he would not have escaped the dreadful bloodshed and loss of many of his comrades. He would more than likely find her dull, she supposed, her life had been so uneventful.

"You have grown quiet, Miss Dalrymple. Shall we discuss the latest affair to rock the *ton*?" he asked quizzically.

"It would be completely one-sided, as I know nothing about them."

"Not a devotee of the scandal sheets? But I see lively curiosity in those fine eyes of yours." He bent slightly, filling her senses with his spicy fragrance. "Are they blue or green? I am intrigued. Green, tonight. In certain circumstances, do they change color, like the ocean driven by tides?" How sensual he made such a commonplace thing as the color of one's eyes.

She found herself smiling foolishly at the compliment. "What circumstances do you refer to?" she asked hastily.

He laughed. "I will leave that for another time."

Another time? Would she see him again? Jo wished her heart hadn't leapt so eagerly.

"Attempting to carry on a conversation while waltzing is an absurdity," she said a trifle coolly. "We should give ourselves up to the pleasure of the dance, do you not think?"

"We might find somewhere quiet?" His murmur was like velvet, making warmth rush up her neck.

"Quieter?" Jo was slightly giddy. "We are at a ball, my lord."

"It's a warm night. The French doors are open, and couples stroll out onto the terrace." She followed his gaze. Some disappeared down the steps into the garden.

Jo's commonsense battled with the desire to venture out onto the terrace with him. What if they were alone? Would he kiss her? She wrestled control over her wayward emotions. "I am claimed for the next dance, Lord Reade."

"I am dismayed to hear it, Miss Dalrymple."

She gazed at his throat, revealed in the space between his cravat and chin. It was rare to find Englishmen with sun-browned skin. Not after a long, frigid winter and a wet English spring. Had he recently been out of the country? Or would he be that color all over? Her eyes widened. What was wrong with her?

"I seem to have caused you some consternation. Was it the prospect of the terrace in the moonlight, or did I tread on your toes?"

There was that humor lurking in his eyes again. As if he guessed her thoughts. She was blushing again, and redheads should *never* blush. How gauche he must find her. It was nonsense, he couldn't have known what she was thinking. "Should you stand on my toes, I would alert you to it immediately."

He bowed his head with mock seriousness. "I appreciate it. You have relieved me."

They exchanged a look of amusement. Then Jo giggled, and he laughed with her.

The orchestra played the slow movement, and the dance ended. Dancing with this man was the most exciting experience of her life. Heavens, her pulse still raced. She would have nothing more to do with Lord Reade. Mr. Ollerton's gentle charm was the safest option, should he continue to show an interest in her.

The baron offered her his arm. "Thank you for the dance, Miss Dalrymple."

"I enjoyed it, sir."

They joined the line to promenade from the dance floor. She prodded her mind for a witty remark that he might laugh at. That he might remember. "Please forgive my lack of entertaining conversation. I struggle to be diverting when slightly breathless."

He gave a deep chuckle. "You held your own admirably, Miss Dalrymple."

They reached her seat where Aunt Mary sat, bowed, and left them.

Had she sounded like a naive schoolroom miss? What did he think of her? But it didn't matter. She was unlikely to see him again.

READE MADE HIS way through the crowd, resisting the temptation for one last view of the pretty debutante. It was just as well Miss Dalrymple refused his offer to stroll on the terrace. It might have led to something more. And he agreed with Letty. Best to leave the young lady to find her perfect match. They had waltzed, and now he should put her from his mind. Difficult, he admired her, she was observant and smart as she attempted to understand him. Not even ladies who experienced far more from life could manage that. But he'd enjoyed her efforts none the less. A little too much.

Reade frowned. It wasn't just that he wanted to slide his hands through the mass of dark red hair and draw her face to his to kiss her soft, wide mouth, it was Miss Joanna Dalrymple's calm demeanor, the kindness he found in her lovely eyes, which drew him. Was he so in need of a woman's compassion that he would put her at risk? He urged himself to stay away. She was not for him. He could only be bad for her.

CHAPTER FIVE

T HE BALL CONTINUED long after the unmasking, and Jo danced a
reel, and the supper dance was still to come.

"I must go to the withdrawing room," Aunt Mary said. "Will you
come, Jo?"

"No, thank you, Aunt. I shall endeavor to attract a footman. My
throat is horribly dry. It's the smoky air."

A footman soon obeyed her summons, offering her a glass of the
ratafia.

As she gratefully sipped the cool liquid, Letty came to join her.
"Did you enjoy your first waltz?"

"It wasn't my first. I waltzed earlier with Mr. Ollerton."

Letty shook her head. "I don't believe I've met the gentleman."

Jo turned to search the crowd for Ollerton, also hoping to see
Reade's head of ebony curls. She spotted him talking again to Mr.
Cartwright. "Lord Reade is not always polite," she said. "I believe he
amused himself by teasing me."

"He is a very attractive man," Letty said, a glimmer in her eyes.
"But not a suitable husband for you, Jo."

"No, he isn't," Jo said. "I did not, for one moment, consider him."

Letty laughed. "Of course you did. Every woman whom he deigns
to give his attention to falls for Reade." She raised her eyebrows. "Did
he invite you to stroll in the gardens with him?"

"Only the terrace," Jo confessed. Was she not worthy of a stroll in the gardens?

"That's perfectly respectable," Letty said. "It's quite crowded on such a warm evening. But I would advise you to refuse any offers to enter the gardens. You might get into trouble."

"What sort of trouble could one face at a ball?"

"Women have been accosted. And sometimes, their reputation in tatters, they are forced to marry someone against their will."

"My goodness."

Despite her determination not to encourage Reade, Jo feared she would have accepted his invitation if he'd persisted. But he had not.

"Not to say Reade would do such a thing. He has no need to."

No, Lord Reade would have his pick of women. Jo had seen the looks cast at him as they danced. "Mr. Forest invited me to take a turn about the gardens, but I declined," Jo said, which had not been difficult. The gentleman had a weak chin and an odd manner of speech.

"That was wise. You are lovely, Jo, and it's conceivable that men are drawn to you. But word has spread that you're an heiress."

Jo gaped. "I? An heiress?"

Letty stared at her. "Surely, you're aware of it?"

Jo thought heiresses hailed from families with vast fortunes. "Papa has recently come into some money, and he sold his business, but..."

Letty put a hand on her arm. "I beg you to be wary of fortune hunters."

"Is Lord Reade a fortune hunter?"

"Heavens, no."

"Then why..."

Letty put a hand on Jo's arm. "There are reasons. I cannot explain." She smiled. "If I said he was a wounded soul, I suspect you would be drawn to such a man, would you not?"

It would be untruthful to deny it. "Do tell me more about him."

Letty tilted her head. "A little perhaps, although I doubt I should."

"Do not be concerned for me, Letty. I merely find him interesting."

"He is that. What can I tell you about him?" Letty tapped her fan on her chin. "He is the only son of the fourth Baron Reade who died earlier this year. Reade's estate lies on the Cumbrian coast."

"Does his family live there?" Jo asked.

"He has no family. I've no idea what condition the estate is in. Reade has set about restoring it. I believe his father did not leave it in good order. As they didn't get on, Reade left straight after university and bought a set of colors in the infantry with money left to him by his mother. A captain, he served under Wellington at Waterloo. The Prince Regent rewarded him generously for his service to the crown."

So, her guess was correct. Reade had been in the army. It fitted, for he appeared to be a man who'd faced danger and seen much of the world. *A wounded soul.* Jo tamped down the desire to know more.

"Reade avoids any romantic entanglements with ladies of the *ton*," Letty said. "I have seen women try to snare him, Jo. None of them captured his heart. He shows no interest in marriage. He is a good friend of Cartwright's and mine, but I see you are interested and must again caution you against him. I should not like to see you hurt."

"He is unlike any man I've ever met," she admitted.

Letty's eyes sparkled. "Men like Reade and Cartwright are fascinating creatures."

It was plain that Letty loved her husband dearly.

"I have decided upon the sort of gentleman I wish to marry," Jo said, "A quiet, sensible, home-loving man. I shall not fall under Baron Reade's spell."

"Oh, dear," Letty said with a smile. "I do hope you change your mind about seeking such a husband."

Unsure of Letty's meaning, Jo glanced around at the elegant guests, drinking champagne and laughing together. "Are there fortune hunters here tonight?"

"Most certainly," Letty said. "And impoverished lords with estates to maintain who must marry for money."

"But that seems so...mercenary," Jo protested. How would she know if a man loved her or just wanted her dowry?

"A marriage of convenience can suit both parties. A man gains a wealthy wife, a woman the title. And sometimes it becomes a love match." She nodded toward a couple who stood close together. "The Wade's marriage was a business arrangement. But see how fond they are of each other," she smiled. "I'm sure London is very different to the country village where you grew up. Wealth, position, and birth rule here. You must try to keep a cool head, Jo. You wish to marry for love, and I can recommend it. But take care. Some gentlemen have a great deal of charm but are not to be trusted. I fear your father and your aunt will not easily see through them because they lack experience of London society." Her expression darkened. "And there is a wicked side to this city one hopes never to see."

She wondered if Letty had seen it. The grave look in her eyes made Jo suspect she might have. She'd love to ask her, and perhaps one day, she would. "Reade gave me a similar warning."

Letty raised her eyebrows. "He did?"

"In a roundabout fashion." He had piqued Jo's curiosity and made her look at the gentlemen around her with fresh eyes. Reade, too. Where did he fit in the scheme of things?

"Don't look so concerned, Jo! I didn't mean to worry you." Letty patted her arm. "Enjoy the pleasures London offers." She opened her reticule and took out a calling card. "This is my address. Please send word should you need someone to talk to."

Jo took it with a nod of thanks. "I am most fortunate to have met you, Letty."

"I am glad we are friends, Jo," she said. "Did you receive an invitation to the Feldman's rout on Saturday?"

"Mrs. Millet mentioned it. What is a rout?"

"Routs are most entertaining. There will be no dancing. Guests cram the reception rooms to indulge in conversation and fine wine. There might be music and card play, with a nice supper."

"It sounds…stifling."

"They are less formal, and one might stroll the gardens on a warm evening." She smiled. "But choose carefully who accompanies you."

Jo must have appeared disheartened, for Letty laughed. "The time will come when you trust a gentleman well enough to place your safety in his hands." She rose. "I must go, the supper dance is about to begin."

Left to her thoughts, Jo wondered how long it would take to meet the man she would marry. To have her future settled. They were to spend only a few months in London, which would pass quickly. And if no suitor she approved of presented himself, like Cinderella, when the clock struck midnight, she would return to Marlborough. It was where her father was happiest. He chafed at the way things were done, saying he never wished to have a valet fussing over him, or an infernal uppity butler, and liked to eat his breakfast in his shirt sleeves. He missed Sooty and feared their dog was pining for them.

Although Jo loved their home and the people she had known all her life, she would be devastated to return, having failed to find a husband. Everyone who knew her, which was the whole village, had wished her well and expected to hear of her marriage. Would she soon be back in her old bedchamber, chatting at church, dancing with dull men at assemblies, and retiring when the chickens went to roost?

She wanted adventure! And she was now accustomed to London hours. It would sadden her father. He would urge her to choose a husband among those in Marlborough who had expressed a wish to marry her. Not one had sparked the remotest interest in her. So few men in London had either, except for Baron Reade and Mr. Ollerton. But Mr. Ollerton had not come to ask her to dance again. Nor had she caught sight of him in the crowd since they danced. He had promised to call on them. She hoped he would.

Lord Hislop came toward her. Jo had promised him the supper dance. She groaned inwardly. Worry creased his face into deep lines, and he perspired heavily. She rose with a smile as he approached.

Her father was leading another lady onto the dance floor. Perhaps it wouldn't be Mrs. Millet, she thought with relief.

READE STOOD WITH Cartwright, his gaze resting on Miss Dalrymple, performing the supper dance with that poor sod, Hislop. She looked pained, for he'd just trodden heavily on her foot. He fought a surprising urge to wrestle her away from the fellow.

"I'm told Virden was here earlier," Cartwright said. "Didn't see him. He never stays long."

Reade shrugged. "Nor I. There must be three hundred people here tonight. I have some news. It appears the bill of sale I found in the Virden's house was couched in vague terms and inconclusive. Although we're pretty sure of what goods it refers to, it wouldn't stand up in a magistrate's court."

"They're sly customers. Been getting away with their dark deeds for some time."

"Let's hope we reel them all in at their meeting near the docks. But the reason for it worries me." He frowned. "It can have only one purpose. We must discover where it is held and quickly. I've assigned Black and Goodridge to follow Virden. I'll relieve them when I'm free from my other commitments."

"The Regent?"

Reade nodded. "We fear there could be another attempt on his life. People have grown even more unsettled since the government enforced its system of economy. While it was to reduce debts caused by the wars and the aftermath of Waterloo, people are starving, and the landowners suffer."

"Fury is mounting since Prinny ignored the government's advice to issue a royal command to abandon all the work on his Brighton pavilion," Cartwright said. "The work goes on unhindered."

"When you think of poor Spencer Perceval shot down by a madman, back in '12, you'd think it would give Prinny pause." Reade shook his head. "But no. We have our work cut out to keep him alive."

"He believes himself invincible, methinks. Did you enjoy your dance with Miss Dalrymple?" Cartwright asked, moving on to a far more pleasant subject.

"I did. But you are unlikely to see it again."

"No? I can't remember seeing you stand up with a debutante before. I liked her. Nothing coquettish or false about her."

"Miss Dalrymple is charming. And quite gorgeous," Reade added thoughtfully, his gaze still resting on her as she entered the supper room with Hislop.

"Then, the reason you won't dance with her again is…?"

"Really, Cartwright. Must I spell it out? A country lass. An innocent with a romantic view of life. Marriage. An orderly existence." His eyes widened. "The refurbishment of Seacliffe in the latest style when I have just been at pains to restore it. Not to mention, outfitting the nursery."

Cartwright stroked his chin. "I'm afraid I can't quite make out your meaning." It was obvious from his smile that he had.

"Shall we find some decent liquor while I explain it to you? You are obviously a dull-witted fellow."

Cartwright chuckled. "An excellent idea. There's a fire and a fine brandy in the library."

"You've already checked?" Reade asked as they left the ballroom.

"Always do. Only way to endure these infernal evenings."

"Then, why come?"

"Because Letty enjoys them."

"Ah-ha!" Reade laughed. "Precisely what I referred to."

"I have no complaints. There are many advantages to marriage you did not mention."

"Apart from the obvious, you can list them over the brandy," Reade said.

"I prefer to keep you intrigued," Cartwright said.

"Who says I'm intrigued?"

"You may have little desire to discover the delights of marriage for yourself, but it's my hope you will reach a point in your life when you do wish it."

Reade was not about to discuss how very unsuited he was to marriage. "I wonder why married men are always so keen to marry off their single friends?"

"Because it will mean you're recovering."

"Recovering?" Reade sighed, but he couldn't fool Cartwright, so he didn't try. "I fear you are about to tell me, and I must urge you to please don't, Brandon."

"I shall restrain myself." They entered the library, and Cartwright headed for the drink's table. He poured them each a glass of brandy, his gaze serious as he offered Reade the glass.

"Good fellow." Reade took a long swig and resolutely pushed the lady's heart-shaped face and big green eyes from his mind. Miss Joanna would find a husband soon enough. A decent fellow, one hoped. The prospect gave him little solace as he took his brandy snifter and wandered over to the fire. His mood had lowered, which happened too often, despite him fighting against it.

He glanced back at Cartwright, who looked to be gearing himself up for another rousing discussion on how marriage could fix all ills. "You didn't happen to discover a pack of cards during your reconnaissance, did you? The card room is unpleasantly crowded. And I dislike watching Alvanley put another nail in the coffin of Underbank Hall."

CHAPTER SIX

J O ROSE LATE, and on her way to breakfast, discovered several calling cards the butler had placed on a silver salver on the hall table. At two o'clock, four gentlemen crowded into their parlor, Lord Hislop, Mr. Ollerton, Mr. Payne, and Mr. Gregson. The two younger gentlemen were not long down from Oxford, their faces earnest and slightly pained. Jo suspected they obeyed their fathers' orders to set themselves up with an heiress. She almost giggled at the thought. Mrs. Millet had done her job too well. Her father was hardly a nabob.

She relished the opportunity to observe Mr. Ollerton's face. Without his mask, he was undeniably handsome. He reminded her of someone, though she couldn't think who it could be for she knew few people in London. His eyes were hazel as she'd guessed, his features finely wrought. He thanked her with his pleasant smile as he accepted an iced cake from the stand. As she passed the teacups around, the aroma of freshly baked pound cake and scones sweetened the air. He and Lord Hislop eyed each other warily, while the other two gentlemen enthused over a pantomime at the Sans Pareil, which Jo had not seen.

She sipped her tea and searched for a way to enliven the gathering. But she'd learned how strictly ordered morning calls were. She couldn't suggest a game of charades or cribbage. A distinctly strained air hovered in the room, despite Aunt Mary's enthusiastic description of their visit to Astley's Amphitheater.

Conversation ambled about. Lord Hislop complained about the wet spring following such a chilly winter. Mr. Ollerton spoke in warm terms of Viscountess Lisle's' triumphant ball, the superiority of the orchestra, the delicious supper. Mr. Payne enthused about how much fun it had been to be in disguise. Jo, weary after little sleep, fought not to yawn.

After the half-hour had passed, the two young gentlemen rose to their feet, obviously as eager to be gone as she was to see them go. Lord Hislop and Mr. Ollerton tarried. Lord Hislop stood and looked pointedly at Mr. Ollerton, who remained seated. Finally, Hislop bowed, scowled at Mr. Ollerton, and left the room after Jo declined his invitation to promenade in the park the following day. She had promised to accompany Aunt Mary to the British Museum to view the famous Elgin Marbles brought from Greece a year ago amidst great controversy.

Aunt Mary, anticipating Ollerton's imminent departure, said goodbye to him and left the room to fetch her knitting.

Mr. Ollerton made no move to leave. In his blue coat, which suited his coloring, he crossed his legs and settled back on the sofa, as if readying himself for a nice long chat. "As soon as they fix the wheel on my curricle, I hope you'll allow me to drive you to the park, Miss Dalrymple."

"I look forward to it." Unsure how to proceed, Jo gestured at the tea tray. "More tea, Mr. Ollerton?"

"Thank you. Just a drop. I must obey the proprieties," he said, making no effort to do so.

She rang for hot water. "What part of England are you from, Mr. Ollerton?"

After Maude brought hot water, Jo busied herself making the tea. She added milk and handed him a cup and saucer, which he took with a slight inclination of his head.

He refused the cake plate with a shake of his head. "I am the second son of Viscount Cranswick of Lancashire, Miss Dalrymple. As my brother, Julian is the heir. I was expected to go into the army, or the church, or study law." His charismatic smile pulled at his lips. "But none appealed to me."

"What will you do?" Jo asked. In her opinion, everyone should work.

"I prefer a simple life. Fortunately, I have inherited some money from my mother. I plan to buy a country property and spend my days there."

"It is wise to plan and work hard to achieve it." She looked up from her teacup and saw him watching her with a speculative expression in his hazel eyes. Was he considering her for his wife? She hoped he wouldn't mention it. She needed more time. Many *ton* marriages, made during the Season, seemed so hasty and cold-blooded.

"And you, Miss Dalrymple?" he asked, putting down the cup. "I hope no gentleman has yet turned your head?"

Jo disliked the question. As if her head could be turned so quickly by any man, she thought, firmly pushing the vision of Reade away. "I have only been in London a short while, Mr. Ollerton," she gently chided.

He placed his cup and saucer on the table, then edged close to take hold of her hand. "I believe I have my answer and can breathe again. I hope we will meet soon. When they've mended my curricle, we can enjoy a ride to the park together."

Jo glanced down at the slim hand, holding hers, wondering if she should withdraw it from his clasp. She didn't wish to be rude, but it seemed rather presumptuous. "We have engagements for the rest of the week. Perhaps the Feldman's rout on Saturday?"

"I haven't received an invitation," he said with a quick frown. "But, I have yet to read my post." He shrugged. "I confess a reluctance to read it, Miss Dalrymple. So much arrives during the Season,

57

invitations, circulars, charities wishing for support." He laughed. "No doubt, my butler will place it under my nose when I return."

Aunt Mary entered the room, her blue eyes behind her glasses exhibiting surprise at still finding him there.

Mr. Ollerton released Jo's hand and stood. "I look forward to seeing you again soon." He bowed. "Miss Dalrymple, Miss Hatton."

Jo rang the bell.

"Mr. Spears is down in the cellar, Miss Jo," Sally said, coming into the room. "May I be of service?"

"Mr. Ollerton is leaving. Bring his hat and cane, please, Sally."

When Sally appeared again, Mr. Ollerton took his things from her with a smile. "Thank you, Sally. I gather from your fresh rosy complexion you hail from the country?

Sally bobbed a curtsey. "Yes, sir. Coventry, sir. I've not been long in London."

He nodded, and with a slight bow, said his goodbyes, and left the house.

Jo went to the window and observed Mr. Ollerton from behind the curtain as he climbed into a hackney. The carriage took off down the road. Moments later, a man on horseback rode in the hackney's wake. At first, she thought the rider had discovered an acquaintance in Mr. Ollerton, but she was mistaken, for he remained several yards behind him until they were out of sight.

"Did I see Mr. Ollerton holding your hand?" Aunt Mary settled into a chair with her knitting bag.

Jo turned. "Yes, he did."

"How outrageous! But you have captured his heart, Jo."

Jo returned to the sofa. "Perhaps."

"Do you like the gentleman?"

"He is genial and attractive." She narrowed her eyes thoughtfully and brushed a crumb from her lace cuff. She had not fallen hopelessly in love with him, but perhaps such a thing didn't happen overnight.

"We shall need to see more of each other. He mentioned a drive in the park when the wheelwright has mended his carriage."

"What about Lord Hislop?"

"A nice man bowed down with worry. His father died recently, and I suspect it has left him in poor circumstances." Jo recalled the worn state of his coat. His shoes lacked a good polish. He would seek a wealthy wife, but it would not be her.

"And the other two gentlemen?"

"I thought them young and silly."

Aunt Mary rummaged in her cloth bag. "But they are a few years older than you, my dear."

"Yes." Jo's thoughts inevitably went to Reade and Mr. Cartwright, who would be in their thirties. "Older men are more interesting, having had so much more experience of life."

"I cannot say I've had much to do with gentlemen, apart from my father and brother, and your father." Aunt Mary's knitting needles flew, the beige wool trailing from her bag. "All decent, upstanding citizens. But it's been my observation women do mature earlier," she added with conviction as the clack of her busy needles filled the room.

To her annoyance, Jo could not agree, for here she was foolishly thinking of the curly black locks and dark brown eyes of the most unsuitable gentleman in London.

IN HIS BEDCHAMBER at Albany, Reade woke when his valet knocked.

"Come." He threw back the covers. Sitting on the edge of the bed, he rubbed the back of his neck. He'd had another nightmare and woken in a sweat. It was always the same dream. Reaching for his pocket watch, he thumbed it open. Nine o'clock. An indecent hour to rise. He ran a hand over his bare chest and yawned.

"You asked me to wake you at nine, my lord," Minshull said. "I have brought your coffee and hot water."

Reade took the coffee from him with a nod of thanks. "What sort of day is it?"

"Rained earlier." His valet went to the window and drew back the curtains, admitting the morning sun into the room. "Clouds have blown away. Promises to be a fine day."

Reade swallowed the last of the rich brew. He had an appointment at Horse-Guards. He'd be at the Regent's beck and call on Friday. Prinny had taken to him, demanding Reade be among his entourage when he ventured out.

At the washstand, Minshull poured more hot water into the basin from the jug.

Reade briskly sponged himself all over with the soap he favored. He washed his hair over the basin, then, with a shiver, rubbed icy water over his face and torso with a sponge. Despite the sun, a cool breeze swept in through the window. He dried himself and rubbed his hair briskly with a towel.

During his years in the army, he'd grown to appreciate a douse of cold water. It helped banish fatigue. But tiredness because of consistently poor sleep didn't stay away for long. He applied shaving soap to his jaw and picked up his razor. His eyes stared back at him groggily. He hadn't slept well since Waterloo. Every night when he rested his head on the pillow, his thoughts took him back there.

Reade brushed his teeth, acknowledging that he did not join with others to relive the battle stories or to glorify the dethroned monarchs and victorious generals. It was the men who had died that he remembered—some who had been with him for years.

He shrugged into his dark gray coat and settled the tall beaver on his head. Pulling on gloves, he walked through to the bay-fronted drawing room. Minshull rattled crockery in the small kitchen. Sometimes he wished for more space but resisted moving into the

London house. This suited his needs. It was comfortable enough but provided no sanctuary from his troubled dreams. But nowhere could. While he yearned to put up his feet and read the books piled on his dresser, he doubted he would ever feel peaceful enough to do so.

Reade strolled to the inn a block away in Piccadilly for breakfast. The dining room filled with the aroma of roasting coffee, warm patrons, and hops, and he washed bacon and eggs down with a mug of ale while perusing the newspaper.

Beyond the window, the street was busy, men wending their way home from a late night at their clubs, women shopping with their maids, a hawker selling clocks. One of Reade's men, Wallace, walked into sight. He raised his hand in welcome and entered the inn dining room.

Reade gestured to a seat. He sawed into his bacon. "Anything new to report?"

"Apparently, Mrs. Virden danced with a Mr. Dalrymple at the Lisle's masked ball."

Reade paused as his stomach muscles constricted. "Dalrymple?"

"Yes, Mrs. Virden seemed on friendly terms with him…" Wallace began.

Reade waved his fork. "I heard you. Let me think." He had not met Dalrymple. But according to his daughter, the lovely Miss Joanna, he was a shopkeeper from Marlborough. It was unlikely there'd be another Dalrymple at the ball. How the devil did the fellow who had been in London for less than a month, according to Miss Dalrymple, meet Mrs. Virden? Or had he known her for some time? "Friendly, were they?"

"Yes. Seemed more than acquaintances."

How had Miss Dalrymple's father come to know the Virdens? Letty had befriended the Dalrymple's and might have some knowledge of them. He pulled out his watch. She was unlikely yet to have risen, and Cartwright, if he had any sense, would be with her.

Reade swiftly banished seeking her opinion. She was too astute not to want to know the whole. And that he was not about to tell her.

"There's one other thing," Wallace said, interrupting his train of thought.

"What is it? Out with it, man," Reade demanded, ignoring that he'd motioned him to be silent a moment earlier.

"Yesterday afternoon, they followed Virden to a house in Upper Brook Street, Mayfair, owned by a Lord Pleasance."

"Don't know the fellow. I will look into it, Wallace," he said. "Any further news, bring straight to me."

Wallace stood and saluted. "Right, Captain Reade."

"Don't salute me," Reade said irritably.

Wallace flushed. "Sorry, sir. Served under you. Old habits die hard."

"You are now engaged in undercover work," Reade said, relenting. "Make it a habit not to go blathering a man's name about. There's a good fellow."

When the man hurried away, Reade called for a coffee.

As he drank, his thoughts returned to Miss Dalrymple. Was it possible she could be in danger? What might the Virdens want with her father? Was he an innocent man caught in their web? It chilled Reade to think it. While he wasn't ready to question Dalrymple, he'd make it his business to find out more about him.

He finished his drink, rose, and tossed coins onto the table. He had an appointment to keep.

CHAPTER SEVEN

O N FRIDAY, JO and Sally went to view the Prince Regent's return to Carlton House from parliament after reading the king's speech. While the sky was overcast, there'd been no sign of rain. Hopeful for fine weather, they positioned themselves on the pavement near Saint James's gardens, crushed in among a rowdy crowd. Jo tried to ignore the unpleasant smell of unwashed bodies. Someone elbowed her hard in the side, but it failed to diminish her excitement.

A ripple of noise rose from the crowd as the Regent's royal coach and his entourage advanced down St. James's Street, the horse guards splendid in their uniforms and the shiny coats of their mounts gleaming.

Sally chatted as the coach came closer. The mutterings and murmurs around them became loud abuse. Men shook their fists, and a few pushed forward toward the coach.

Nervous, Jo glanced around. "Stay close to me, Sally." The shouting and raised voices drowned out Jo's words.

Drawn by six peerless white horses, the glossy, black royal coach, elaborately decorated in gold with red wheels, drew level to where they stood. Jo barely had a moment to admire it when a handful of gravel splattered against the coach door, tossed by someone in the crowd to the right of her. The horses sidled nervously as the horse-guards broke ranks and rode toward the people, seeking the assailant.

Fearing they'd be trampled, Jo pulled Sally back, but like a surging sea, the crowd spread in all directions.

Jo kept a grip on Sally's arm, her stomach in knots. "We must leave."

They came up against a wall of people. They had only moved a few paces through the seething mob, when a loud bang, followed closely by another, rent the air. A far side window of the royal coach shattered, glass shards flying over the road. As screaming rent the air, His Royal Highness stared out, seemingly unharmed. For a moment, there was silence, and then a rumble of panic-stricken people.

"Oh, miss, was that a pistol shot?" Sally cried as they struggled to move on. "Is it a revolution? We must get away!"

The horse guards rode into the crowd, their mounts pushing the panicked people back. Barely able to escape a horse's hooves, Jo lost hold of Sally's hand, and the surge of people carried the maid away with them.

Jo tried to follow, but was caught up and dragged in the opposite direction. Finally, free, she was pressed against a brick wall near the entrance to a narrow alley.

Jo searched for Sally amongst the dispersing crowd but didn't see her. Winded, she leaned against the brick wall and tried to keep out of the way of those rushing past. A man tripped and cannoned into her, pushing her backward. Her head banged against the bricks, and she sank dizzily down. Once her head cleared, she struggled to her feet to stare into the shadowy laneway. Was it a way out? It looked forbidding, and she had no idea where it led. But she just couldn't stay here. She stepped inside.

A man watched her from the shadows. Her heart beating, Jo backed away and returned to the fray. Where was Sally? Was she hurt? With gritty determination, despite another bout of dizziness and a stinging forehead, she pushed her way into the surging mass of frightened people, who still ran in all directions.

Jo realized she was in trouble when she'd only taken a few steps. The crowd was too strong for her, and they pulled her off her feet.

An arm looped around her waist and scooped her up, robbing her of breath. Fear rushed through her, her protest muffled against a hard chest. "Put me down."

"You can't stay here."

Jo tried to see who it was but could only see the hard edge of the man's jaw. She squirmed in his arms with panicked breaths as she inhaled his clean scent. A hand clutching his steely shoulder, her palm pressed against the gold buttons on his silk waistcoat, feeling the unresistant hard muscle and bone beneath. Well, he was a gentleman at least and not one of those hollow-chested, pale men she met at balls. Growing desperate, she shoved again, harder, and looked up into his face.

"Lord Reade!" His eyes dark, his mouth pressed in a firm line. "This is hardly necessary. I can walk!" Jo shouted, trying to make herself heard above the clamor swirling around them.

"Don't be foolish." His deep voice rumbled against her ear as he dove through a gap in the eddying mob. People seemed to scatter in his wake.

"I am *not* foolish," she cried. "I am quite capable of taking care of myself."

"So, it would appear. Your forehead is bleeding. What the devil are you doing here?"

What else would she be doing here? "I came to see the Prince of Wales and the royal procession."

He didn't slow his determined stride. "Someone fired on the Regent."

"Well, it wasn't me."

"I'm relieved to hear it."

"Mind where you're going!" A man growled as Reade elbowed past him. He blanched at Reade's expression and hastily moved aside.

"Where are you taking me? I've lost my maid," Jo yelled. "And, you are stifling me."

He rearranged her in his arms, tossing her as if she weighed nothing more than a bag of feathers. But at least her head was now on a level with his. She clung to his shoulder and cast a sideways glance at his fine profile. His dark eyes searched ahead, hard as flint. Jo loathed depending on him, although she'd seen women and children knocked over.

She'd always considered herself indomitable. It had never occurred to her how easily someone like Reade could overpower her. If it were any other man, she would be scared witless, but she was not afraid of Reade. "Something bad could have happened to my maid, Sally. I must find her quickly," she said in a more reasonable tone as she studied a glossy black lock flopping onto his forehead. She could smell his skin, his spicy soap.

"Your maid will find her way," he said grittily. "If you'd been dragged into that alley, something nasty could have happened to you."

"But you have kindly prevented that, so you can put me down now."

"Be patient. Not a virtue of yours, I suspect, Miss Dalrymple."

"Oh, how unfair..." She clamped down her lips when a woman ahead of them staggered after being viciously shoved.

Reade mounted the half-dozen steps to the front door of a building. He placed her on her feet on the narrow porch. She bent to rearrange her skirts, which had ridden up her legs. Her head throbbed. Pressed against his muscular body while breathing in his male scent had shaken her almost as much as the attack on the prince regent.

"Hold still." He framed her face in large, capable hands and studied the wound on her forehead. "It's not too bad. I doubt it will scar and mar your beauty."

She held her breath. Did he find her beautiful? His palms were warm against her skin, his eyes the color of dark chocolate, rimmed with thick black lashes. Up close, he looked less overbearing...somehow more vulnerable. Reade vulnerable? Ridiculous.

Reade pulled a handkerchief from his pocket and offered it to her. "Are you dizzy?"

"No," she lied. She was a little, but she feared he would carry her if she admitted to it.

Dabbing her forehead with the linen square, she decided it was he who made her dizzy, for Reade acting concerned and gentle with her made her knees wobbly. Had she hit her head harder than she thought? She reluctantly dragged her gaze from his to look around the street. Bewildered people were wandering about like lost lambs. Pitiful cries rent the air as they called for lost loved ones. It made her eyes tear up. She stiffened and bit her lip hard. This was no time to weaken. She had to find Sally. "I am grateful for your assistance, Lord Reade," she said, fighting to regain her equilibrium. "Please don't let me keep you. I'll search for my maid."

"Wait a while," he cautioned.

"Was the regent hurt?"

"I don't believe so."

She craned her neck and tried to see what was happening farther down the road. The royal guard had left the chaotic scene. She turned back to Reade. "I will be all right. I doubt anyone is interested in me."

"You think not?" His gaze casually took measure of her. "What's in that silk reticule? Money? Those are fine clothes. And I'll wager the locket is gold. Prime pickings for a pickpocket. You're young enough to attract a procuress in the area. They could have had you away down that alley before anyone was the wiser, and don't think they wouldn't."

Alarmed, she studied his hard face. "What is a procuress?"

"They are women who snare innocent country girls by offering them what they think are respectable jobs."

"What sort of jobs?"

"Something too good to be true. Their goal is to make the girls a prisoner in brothels and sometimes send them overseas. They search for girls at playhouses, coffee shops, and other public places, and have the men who work for them nab them off the streets. They sell young women to their gentlemen clients. The girls are then trapped in brothels for the rest of their lives," he continued, ignoring Jo's horrified gasp. "It's a lucrative business. Female pimps have few morals. They prefer to offer a variety of women, virgins especially, who can fetch anything from a guinea to a hundred guineas."

As he spoke, his gaze remained on the crowd, which was just as well for his unemotional but terrifying revelation made her mouth drop open. "I...would never succumb to a woman like that, no matter what she offered me."

"They might not seek your opinion," he said bluntly, turning, at last, to observe her, his eyes flinty.

Jo shivered and held back from accusing him of exaggeration after a man paused to give her a studied look. Then there was the man in the alley. She could hardly argue the point when Reade would know far more of the evils of a big city than she.

Perhaps he took pity on her for his mouth softened. "I merely make you aware that this is London, Miss Dalrymple. Life here differs vastly from your country town."

"I am aware of it. It seemed perfectly safe to come here. You can hardly accuse me of venturing into the Seven Dials."

He acknowledged it with a nod. "But even in Westminster, there is danger."

Jo thought of Sally and gasped. Had she fallen into the hands of one of those women? She gripped the lapel of his coat. "Lord Reade, please. Can we look for Sally?" She meant to plead with him, but it sounded more like a demand.

"Which way did she go?"

"I...I didn't see." They were now in Bridge Street, which led onto the Westminster Bridge. She pointed back toward James's Park. "They pulled Sally in that direction."

"People fear arrest and are leaving," he said. "It appears safe enough now." He took a firm hold of her hand, and they descended the steps. "I doubt your Sally will have gone far. She will look for you."

His big hand wrapped around hers in a comforting grip. Jo walked beside him past Queen's Garden into Stafford Street. There were small groups huddled on the side of the road, but Sally was not among them. Jo quickened her pace to keep up with his long stride. Didn't it occur to him that her legs weren't as long as his? She hated to think she was a nuisance, something he wished to deal with quickly. He must have somewhere to go. Something important to do. She drew in a deep breath to calm herself and admitted how fortunate she was that Reade had come to her aid. It was distressing to see bewildered folk sprawled on the ground, some weeping and in pain.

"Why are the people so angry with the regent?" Jo asked as her bonnet tipped forward over her forehead. Impossible to push it into position with his powerful grip on her hand and her reticule clutched in the other. He surged ahead like a boat she'd seen on the Thames, driven by a high wind.

"My bonnet!" Jo cried, reduced to pleading.

Reade released her hand. "Hold still."

He bent his knees slightly and rearranged her hat. As if she couldn't do it for herself. He was such a complex man. She subtly studied him at close quarters. When he wasn't glowering, it was such an appealing face, with his straight nose and high cheekbones. What was she doing? He probably knew a great deal about a woman's apparel. Would she never be able to think in his company? She should thank him, walk on, and leave him. Take control of the search herself. But before she could put some distance between them, he caught her hand up in his again.

"People have good reasons for dissatisfaction with the government and with royalty," he said, replying to the question she'd forgotten she'd asked, without lessening his punishing stride. "I don't intend to go into it here."

Meaning he wouldn't tell her.

Jo was in danger of a breathless collapse when a golden head appeared among a group a few yards ahead. "There she is! There's my maid, Sally!"

"Right." He shouldered his way through, pulling her with him.

He released her hand at last, and Jo rushed forward.

"Sally, I was so worried something awful had happened to you."

"I'm so glad you're safe, Miss Jo. A kind gentleman assisted me. He offered to take me home, but I told him I had to help this little boy who is ever so distressed." She stroked the blond head of the wailing child. About six years old, he had a dirty face but seemed otherwise unhurt. "Poor Sam has lost his mother."

"Never mind, lad, we'll find her." Reade knelt to address the boy, a hand on his shoulder. "What's your mother's name?"

"'err name's Alice Crawley," Sam said with a shuddering sob.

Reade stood and shouted Alice's name. His deep voice echoed around the buildings. Those wandering the street turned to stare at them.

A woman in an apron hurried over to them. "I know 'er. Alice works at the inn near 'ere." She gestured with an arm. "Saw 'er up that way, 'round the corner."

Reade hoisted the boy onto his shoulders and strode off with Jo and Sally hurrying behind him.

They turned the corner.

"Ma!"

Sam's mother perched on a step in a lane that ran down beside the barracks. Alice held her handkerchief to her cheek. Blood dribbled down her neck. Reade put Sam down, and the boy ran and threw himself into her arms.

"Sam!" She gathered him up with a sob.

Reade shrugged off Jo's effusive thanks as they continued along the street.

"People will be rounded up and questioned," he said. "You don't want to be here when that happens. I cannot accompany you home, but I will see you safely into a hackney."

"We are most grateful," Jo said, chagrined for her earlier disparaging thoughts.

They entered a busy thoroughfare, and he flagged a hackney carriage. When it pulled up, Jo gave the jarvey the address in Upper Brook Street, Mayfair.

Reade stared at her for a long moment. He opened the carriage door. "Remember what I told you. You can't just wander around London unescorted. Your maid can hardly protect you in situations like this." He assisted them both inside. "You, too, Miss Sally. Country girls come to London and fall into the wrong hands," he said. "The brothels are full of them."

Sally blanched.

Jo glared at him, shocked at his bluntness. She was grateful for his help, but that was unnecessary. There was no need to alarm Sally. Jo's benevolent attitude toward him evaporated. Surely there was no need to point out how naive and foolish she'd been. "Thank you for your help, sir," she said stiffly.

An amused light sparked in Reade's eyes. He shut the door and doffed his hat as the carriage pulled away.

"Well, that was quite an adventure, wasn't it miss?" Sally fell back against the squab.

"I wasn't aware the prince regent was so unpopular," Jo said. "I only had a glimpse of him and the other gentleman beside him." What she'd seen of the Regent disappointed her: a sulky, fleshy face, and plump body in an overly ornate coat. But she was pleased that he didn't appear hurt.

"It's the way he goes on, and the government, too. We're worse off than we might have been if Napoleon had won the war." Sally wrinkled her freckled nose. "You'll feel more the thing when you get home and have a nice hot cup of tea."

"I'm sure I will."

The hackney entered the quiet Mayfair streets, the air fragrant with spring foliage and blossoms spilling over walls in the mansion gardens. Jo barely looked at the elegant houses they passed while she mused over how Reade could affect her emotions to such a degree. She basked in the warmth of approval from his dark eyes and hated his criticism so much she rushed to defend herself. And when he laughed at her, her fingers itched to slap him.

Sally glanced at her. "You were lucky the gentleman came to your aid, Miss Jo."

"That I was," she admitted.

"And so handsome, too," Sally said with a gusty sigh.

"Do you think so?" Jo said, drawing in a breath. "I hardly noticed."

Sally raised her fair eyebrows. "All that black hair. And those muscles! Hard to miss 'em."

"Let us put the unpleasant episode behind us," Jo said firmly.

"Yes, miss. Not as though we'll see him again, do you think?"

"I daresay I might at some affair or other, but only in passing, Sally."

She wondered if he would attend the rout as the hackney pulled up outside the townhouse. "And here we are." She smiled at the maid. "That was exciting, wasn't it? No need to mention it to my father or my aunt."

"No, miss."

But Jo suspected when she and Reade met again, there would not be a polite exchange of pleasantries. Something had changed between them. There was a beguiling raw power about him, but also a vulnerability that drew her even more. She allowed herself to dream but knew it was foolish to imagine a life with him. The vision of Reade sitting in a drawing room with a napkin on his knee, sipping tea, and speaking of his hopes and dreams made her smile and shake her head.

READE TURNED AWAY as the hackney cab rattled down the road, taking Miss Dalrymple back to the safety of Mayfair. It shook him up to find her in such a dire situation. This investigation stripped his emotions raw and sickened him because it involved vulnerable young women like her. She'd been vulnerable in that mob, but still placed her maid's safety before her own. She proved herself not only to be brave but good-hearted. Just the sort a man would want for his wife. A delectable armful was Miss Joanna. She was feisty. She'd objected to his strong-arm tactics and scoffed at his warning. Her lovely eyes flashed darts at him.

A reluctant grin tugged at his lips as he signaled to a hackney to take him to Whitehall. They would question those they'd rounded up after the attack on Prinny. But he doubted they'd find the culprit. He would have been long gone. Pebbles couldn't shatter a window, nor was it a gunshot, for there was no sign of gunpowder. More would be known once they'd examined the coach.

An hour later, having learned nothing more, Reade entered through the columned marble foyer of Carlton House. As soon as he reached the crest of the curving staircase, he heard the regent's raised voice from the Blue Room.

He knocked and entered. Seated at his desk, a group of anxious gentlemen surrounded Prinny as he espoused his opinions. Few would risk criticizing the regent.

James Murray, Prinny's Aide-de-camp, who traveled with him when the attack occurred, had been summoned to the Commons to give evidence.

A few minutes later, news came that Murray's recounting of events confirmed Reade's opinion. It was not a gun because two small holes about a quarter of an inch apart revealed no trace of gunpowder, and they found no shot. An air gun most likely.

Prinny was full of bluster, ignoring evidence and passing the incident off as some miscreant throwing stones. But after such a violent display from the public, he sank into a foul mood, blaming Sidmouth's circular suppressing all seditious publications for the rise of discontented people. Prinny dismissed the accusation that his lavish spending and overindulgence in these troubled times were acting like salt rubbed in a wound.

"We will hold a fete," he said. "Open Carlton House grounds to the people."

"But your highness," one of his lackey's protested, "we held a fete a few months ago."

Reade clamped down his teeth. Hardly a suitable solution. While the poor went hungry and nothing was done to improve their lot, more events like this and possibly worse would happen.

"Reade!" Prinny's gaze settled on him. He beckoned him forward.

"Your highness." Reade bowed deeply.

"What news?" Prinny waved his hands at the rest of the men. "Get out, all of you."

When the door closed on the last of them, Reade said, "We need to pursue the matter. Find the culprit to settle down the rumors."

Prinny shrugged. "Storm in a teacup."

"We must double the guard."

"No. Make no changes." Prinny stared into the distance. "The people wish to see me. Let them do so."

His attitude didn't surprise Reade. Despite the indulgent way he lived, Prinny was not one to fuss over an attack on his life. "What have you discovered concerning these missing women?"

"We have two strong suspects. They are being followed."

Prinny nodded. "I rely on you to bring this swiftly to an end."

Finally dismissed, Reade wondered again about Prinny's interest and why this became a matter for the Home Office instead of Bow Street. He knew better than to ask the regent. No doubt, the answer would come when the villains were all either dead or imprisoned.

He went home to change for the formal dinner he was to attend that evening, thinking of Miss Joanna Dalrymple, who lived in Upper Brook Street. A coincidence? Or something more? Should he be worried about her? It would be wise to look out for her. Cartwright would accuse him of falling for the lady. It would please his friend to believe it, but Reade had no intention of it.

CHAPTER EIGHT

THE FELDMAN'S ROUT was just as Letty described. Beautifully dressed guests crammed the reception rooms, gathered around the men who enthralled them with their witty repartee.

The air was humid with an occasional rumble of thunder in the distance, but it had not yet rained. Such a crush made the rooms unpleasant, the atmosphere heavily laden with scent and sweat. Jo longed to escape for a breath of fresh air.

Mr. Cartwright and her father went into the salon to play a game of whist. Letty's husband seemed to have taken to him, for they shared an enthusiasm for farming. Although her father no longer owned any land, he had an excellent knowledge of farming practices.

Aunt Mary had found an old friend. They'd been debutantes together many years ago and now sat discussing the famous scandals that rocked the *bon ton* back when they were young.

Jo's new acquaintance, Charlotte Graham, did not appear. Jo knew none of the smartly dressed guests, but she refused to cling to the Cartwrights. After Letty's mama-in-law joined them, Jo excused herself to wander the rooms, attempting to look as if she had a purpose and a place to go. A string quartet competed with the vociferous guests. There was to be no dancing, which Jo considered a dreadful waste of fine music.

Mr. Ollerton must not have received an invitation, for he was not here tonight. Neither was Lord Reade. Did she regret Reade's absence more than Ollerton's? Jo chewed her bottom lip. She was losing focus. The plan she'd conceived for a contented, quiet life no longer seemed to appeal. But she must give Mr. Ollerton a chance, should he wish it. They had hardly spoken, for he seldom appeared at the same social gatherings as she did. And they were yet to drive to the park.

Routs were not her favorite entertainment, Jo decided as she fanned herself and scanned the crowd one more time for anyone she knew.

In the supper room, a lavish display of dishes awaited the guests, but it was too hot to eat. Jo took a glass of cider from a footman's tray.

As the evening progressed, the heat seemed to worsen. Some of the candles drooped in the silver candelabrum. The drink had done little to cool her. She entered the drawing room, where many guests gathered. Some wandered out through the French doors onto the terrace.

A refreshing breeze drew Jo to the door. The gardens looked mysterious and beautiful in the lantern light. Could she roam the garden paths alone? There were people doing just that. Perhaps if she didn't go far?

Jo was outside before she knew it and gratefully inhaling the cooler, leaf-scented air.

Guests gathered at the far end of the terrace, engaged in heated disagreement. Something to do with the prime minister and a pamphlet. It was awkward standing alone. Jo feared they might think she was eavesdropping. She descended the steps into the garden, where well-ordered paths led off through clipped hedges and shrubbery.

A couple laughingly made their way back toward the house and glanced curiously at her as they passed. Jo lowered her head and hurried on. She approached a break in the trees and emerged onto a freshly scythed lawn to find a large fountain filled with waterlilies and lit by two braziers. Even the sight of water was refreshing. "Would anyone mind if I took off my slippers and stockings and cooled my feet?" she murmured with a smile, admiring the marble statue of some Roman god at its center.

"I wouldn't object, Miss Dalrymple. Please do."

She had thought herself alone. When Jo turned, Lord Reade stood before her in his black and white evening clothes, laughter in his eyes. She drew in a sharp breath, annoyed at how pleased she was to see him. "Does it amuse you to sneak up on people, sir?"

He grinned. "The grass muffled my footsteps. I'm sorry if I alarmed you. I admit to being tempted to remain silent, however. In hope, you might lift your skirts and wade in the fountain."

Jo bit her lip to stop from smiling. "I had no intention of it."

"An unpleasantly hot evening, is it not? The water looks cool. Shall we do it together? Or do you think there are fish in it?"

Jo giggled. "You are absurd, sir."

His smile seemed to invite her to take part in something even more risqué. Jo's face grew hot, but fortunately, it was too dark for him to see. "We may still get wet," she said inanely. "It's so hot it must surely rain."

He glanced up at the clouds drifting over the sky. "There's a storm somewhere, but it's far off. I believe we are safe. You appear to be alone. Might I walk with you?"

"I'm not sure I want to go farther."

Deeper into the gardens? She should go back. Would he take advantage of the shadows to steal a kiss? Jo moistened her lips, admitting she would like him to kiss her. A stolen kiss had no real importance, apparently, here in London. The scandal sheets she'd been able to get her hands on shocked her. Couldn't she trust him to behave like a gentleman? He had come to their aid during the attack on the Royal Coach. She hesitated. *Or could it be that she was unsure of herself?* Minutes ticked by while he waited for her answer.

His laugh was low and inviting, sending electricity racing along her nerve endings.

"I can almost see the wheels turning in that pretty head of yours, Miss Dalrymple. Am I to learn what you have decided?"

Jo struggled to take control of herself. She did not want him to know how easily he could affect her, and she suspected he didn't miss much. "Thank you. I caught sight of a gazebo somewhere ahead of us."

"Then you do wish for my company?" he asked with a teasing smile.

"I do." She took his proffered arm.

"It was just that you appeared undecided."

She breathed in his familiar smell, the fine material of his sleeve smooth beneath her gloved fingers. "But, I have decided as you see."

He chuckled low in his throat. It seemed to rumble through her, warm and desirable. She wanted to laugh with him but held herself back.

They walked on.

"You seem not to have suffered any effects from that business concerning the Prince Regent," he said. "I trust I am right?"

"Yes, thanks to you. Nor did my maid. Have they found the person who shot at the royal coach?"

"I don't believe so."

They strolled beneath a majestic flowering tree, the air scented with sweet blossom. "What a magnificent specimen," Jo observed. The crabapple reminded her of her garden at home.

"I am flattered."

She gave a gurgle of amusement. "I referred to the tree." Reade was being deliberately provocative tonight. She would like to think he came to find her because he liked to be with her but couldn't quite believe that was all it was. She suspected he did nothing without an aim. The thought slightly unnerved her.

"Then, I am cut to the quick."

She smiled. "I believe you shall recover, my lord."

"Reade."

She nodded, wondering what he meant by such intimacy. They strolled on through the gardens beneath the flickering lanterns. They were not entirely alone. Other couples with the same aim had deserted the overheated house. The air was soft and pleasant, a slight breeze swaying the branches.

"It's a wonderful garden," Jo said for want of something to break the silence which had settled between them.

"It is a pleasant facsimile of nature. Not equal to the countryside." He strolled, not rushing her off her feet this time. "Living in a polluted city has its drawbacks. Once the heat of the summer arrives, most leave the city for the country."

He sounded disillusioned. Did he prefer the country? She'd thought him a man more suited to town life. She glanced up at him, curious to know what lay behind his words. But attempting to read his thoughts was impossible. She was sure now that he had a reason to be here beyond escaping the heat of the house, and it was not to pay his attentions to her. Something weightier had crept into their conversation. She imagined she'd learn what it was soon enough.

The path led them to a stretch of lawn, silvery in the moonlight. Reade paused, a foot on the step leading up to an ornate gazebo. He went no further, as two people occupied it, standing close together. "Your father leased Lord Pleasant's house for the Season?"

Astonished, she stared at him. "Yes. Why do you ask?" *What interest could it possibly be to him?*

They stepped out of the shadows, and she saw that impenetrable expression on his face again. To understand him felt like attempting to scale a high stone wall.

"Why did your father come to London?"

She scowled at him. "Does he need a reason?" She'd been right, she thought, disappointed. He was not here to steal a kiss. But what? Her chest grew tight. To learn something from her. "We came for my debut."

"And only that?"

"Isn't that reason enough?" she asked, eyeing him. Disliking his silence, she continued, "My father inherited some money. He always hoped to honor his promise to my mother for me to make my Come-out. Mama considered it important. She came from a good family."

"Where did this newfound wealth come from?"

She gaped at him. What business was it of his? She was so flabber-gasted, she rushed to her father's defense. "He was the beneficiary of a distant relative's will. You might consult our solicitor if you doubt us."

He ignored her, not doubt considering her outburst unreasonable. "Your father has been to London before?"

"Many times, I imagine. But some years ago. Why do you ask?"

The couple abandoned the gazebo. Laughing together, they came toward them on the path. After they passed, Reade took her arm and drew her reluctantly along with him up the rise. "I apologize for these questions, but I need to know."

"You might tell me why," she said again. "My family must be the most uninteresting people in London. My father is a decent man," she added grittily.

"I don't doubt he is."

"You are most mysterious, Lord Reade."

"I fear you must find me so."

Jo scowled at him. "I do."

They had entered the gazebo. Reade leaned his back against the rail, his eyes resting on her. How graceful he was, his long limbs arranged in a casual pose. Except that he was more like a tightly wound spring, she thought distractedly. And this was not a casual conversation between two guests at a party. What might he possibly want from her?

"Tell me more about your father. How long did he have the haberdashery store?"

She turned away from his penetrating gaze. It made her nervous and defensive.

Gripping the rail in her gloved fingers, she gazed out over the gardens, a web of luminescent light and shadow where the lamps and moonlight couldn't reach. "Papa bought a farm after he left the navy, but his injured back made such work difficult. He had fallen from the mast onboard ship when he was young. He sold the farm and bought the shop ten years ago." Her polite voice defied her churning thoughts. As if she chatted to the vicar after church. But a sense of foreboding sent a warning to her brain.

"How do you know the Virdens?"

She swung around to face him. "The Virdens? Who are they?"

"You claim not to know Virden?" He sounded skeptical.

"No. I've never met the man. Should I have? Is it important?"

He had moved closer, his eyes searching hers. "Perhaps not," he said inscrutably.

"Then I am relieved, for I cannot supply you with the answers you seek and feel as if I've been playing a rather poor game of charades."

He laughed. "Then, I apologize again."

"I should like you to tell me what lies behind this inquisition."

He huffed out a laugh. "Is it as bad as that?"

"It is confusing and disturbing."

"I'm afraid I'm not at liberty to reveal my reasons. Shall we return to the house?"

Jo narrowed her eyes at him. "Very well." She didn't want to go back. She wanted to question him further about his interest in her father. But it would be a waste of time.

Descending the slope, they walked in silence until they reached the pretty water feature set in the carpet of green lawn. Moonlight made diamond ornaments of the water droplets as they fell. Jo watched them, attempting to order her thoughts.

"It's a shame," Reade murmured close beside her.

A frisson of awareness rose up her neck. "What is?" She turned, caught by the softer note in his voice.

"A beautiful night, a beautiful lady." His voice was seductive, making heat ripple under her skin. "Any man in his right mind would steal a kiss."

"Perhaps you're not in your right mind, sir," Jo said, fighting desire while still unsettled about his questioning. "I can make no sense of you tonight."

He tilted her chin up with his palm. His thumb slid along her jaw, leaving a trail of warmth. She stilled, and her lips parted.

"It will all come to light, eventually."

Jo swallowed. "What will?"

He dropped his hand. "The truth, Miss Dalrymple."

"I think we should return to the house," Jo said, turning away.

"Yes. Regrettably, I must agree with you."

Suddenly furious with him, she balked at taking his arm but was obliged to when a group of people appeared on the path.

Really, the man was impossible! She had been right in her first assessment of Reade. He was involved in something serious and possibly dangerous. But what on earth had her father to do with any of it? Did he think she hid something from him? That if he'd kissed her, she would reveal it? But he changed his mind. Decided he would learn nothing from her. It was insulting. She was not a fool. She wanted to demand Reade tell her what lay behind his questioning, but there was no point. He was as mysterious as the Pyramid of Cheops.

After they reached the terrace, Jo dropped her hand from his arm as if it burned her. "Thank you for your company, Lord Reade. I enjoyed the garden." A group turned to observe them. Let them think what they liked, she thought crossly. "And for such an enlightening conversation."

Reade raised an eyebrow, bowed, and left her.

Jo entered the house and went in search of her father. He'd finished his card game and now sat with Aunt Mary.

Jo hurried over to him. "Papa, do you know a Mr. Virden?"

"That's odd. Mr. Cartwright just asked me the same thing. I've never met the fellow.

"Is he here tonight?" Did you want me to meet him?"

"No, Papa."

"What is this all about, Jo?" Aunt Mary asked.

"I don't know, but Lord Reade seemed to think Papa knew him," Jo said. "He is obviously mistaken."

"Yes. My memory for names is excellent. I would remember Mr. Virden," her father said. "We must find our hostess and thank her for such a pleasant evening. Aunt Mary wishes to retire. She is a little weary."

"Yes, I am too, Papa. I will say goodnight to Letty and Mr. Cartwright."

There was no sign of Reade as she made her way through the reception rooms. She would have enjoyed demanding he apologize for grilling her in that fashion, now that she was certain he'd been wrong. But it gave her pause, for why did he think it?

READE WENT IN search of Cartwright to discover if he'd had better luck with Dalrymple than Reade had done with his daughter. He understood why Miss Dalrymple had been angry and defensive for her father's sake. It was regrettable. He wished he could ease her mind, but he needed to know why Virden visited their home. It seemed clear Joanna knew nothing about Virden. The alternative that she might and was covering up for her father didn't bear thinking about. Reade dismissed the notion. He didn't want to believe she was capable of doing that. But he must not allow her allure to cause him to lose focus.

Dammit, he still wanted to kiss away the worry he'd seen on her pretty face. But one kiss might lead to more, and then where would he be? Far wiser, surely to leave Miss Joanna Dalrymple alone wherever possible.

And he fully intended to do so.

"I mentioned the man's name and drew a blank," Cartwright said. "He either doesn't know him, or he has the best poker face in London."

Who was Virden meeting at Lord Pleasant's house? At some stage, Reade would need to confront Joanna's father with the evidence of Virden's comings and goings and demand an explanation as unpalatable as this would be.

It was frustrating how every avenue led them to a dead end. There was no evidence pointing to the man behind this gang. If they didn't get him, he could continue to operate even with the rest of them in jail. It was not these few felons they were after. They wanted their leader, who had tentacles that stretched far beyond England's shores.

CHAPTER NINE

AUNT MARY WAS unwell with a headache the next day. Jo's father was engaged in writing letters home, hoping for news about the new owner of the shop and Sooty.

Idleness never appealed to Jo, and as the efficient staff took care of everything, she decided on an excursion to the Pantheon Bazaar in Oxford Street. Surely even Reade would not consider it reckless, as she and Aunt Mary had visited Piccadilly without harassment a few days earlier. Elegant carriages had filled the street while well-dressed women browsed the shops with their liveried servants.

Jo descended from the hackney with Sally onto Oxford Street, right outside the splendid building of the Pantheon Bazaar. Exotic smells greeted them as they walked into the grand entry with a high arch above. Any lingering doubt Reade might have instilled in her vanished as they joined the others roaming the shops. Every sort of item one could wish for was on display, novelties, jewelry, and furs. Jo tried on a becoming wide-brimmed hat trimmed with cerulean blue ribbons and promptly bought it, together with a straw bonnet decorated with artificial primroses for Sally to wear to church.

Another hour passed as they purchased more items. When Jo opened her coin purse to pay for a tortoiseshell comb decorated with pearls, she found she only had enough money left for the hackney ride home. She put the comb down and closed her purse.

"I have never seen the like of these shops, Miss Jo," Sally said, who seemed thrilled with her new hat.

"I intend to come back soon," Jo said, admiring the wares in shops as they passed. They carried the milliners' hat boxes and their other packages through the bazaar, searching for the way out. The arched windows revealed the lowering sun above the rooftops. How quickly the hours had passed. Her father would be anxious.

She spied a door leading outside. "We'd best find a hackney."

The street was unfamiliar. "This is not Oxford Street, where we came in." She spied a signpost. "It's Marlborough Street." There were no hackneys in sight. "We might have better luck around the corner where there's a hackney stop."

They passed young gentlemen who lounged about in conversation or sauntered up and down. Dressed in tight coats, some wore canary-yellow trousers, others striped waistcoats, their cravats elaborate creations.

"My father calls them coxcombs," Jo murmured.

A gentleman with a purple and yellow paisley waistcoat raised his quizzing glass to ogle them.

Jo flushed. "How rude," she said under her breath, frowning at a gentleman whose collar was so high he could barely turn his head. He still viewed their progress as they hurried along.

Loaded up with parcels, they reached the corner. Jo breathed more easily when a hackney appeared at the top of the street. "Wait here with the boxes, Sally. I'll hail that jarvey."

The jarvey ignored her and drove his horse past. Jo dropped her arm. Several vehicles passed up and down the busy street. When another hackney appeared, Jo, determined not to let him escape, rushed onto the road. She waved her handkerchief as the carriage advanced down the street, the horse at a fast trot.

The jarvey drew his horse to a stop some yards further along. Jo hurried to give him directions. When she turned back, there was no sign of Sally. Their hat boxes and parcels were still on the pavement where she'd left them. Fancy leaving them like that. Annoyed, Jo ran over and gathered them up, expecting Sally to emerge from a shop. She'd barely turned her back for a minute. Where had the girl got to?

The jarvey yelled at her. He was losing his patience. Jo smiled sweetly and held up her hand, then darted into a nearby shop. She came out a few minutes later, none the wiser. The shopkeeper had not seen Sally.

Jo ran to where the men still loitered about and approached the exquisitely dressed young gentleman in the purple and yellow waistcoat who dabbed at his mouth with a lace-edged handkerchief.

"Have you seen my maid, sir?"

He waved the handkerchief, releasing a cloying scent. "Yes."

"Quickly. Tell me! Where did she go?"

He grinned. "She walked around the corner into Oxford Street with you."

The man standing next to him guffawed.

"Oh!" With a glare, Jo ran back to where she'd last seen Sally, gasping, boxes dropping from her nerveless fingers. Sally had not returned. Now thoroughly alarmed, Jo retraced her steps, her throat tight. What could have happened to her? It was as if she'd disappeared into thin air.

With a curse, the jarvey drove on, leaving Jo alone, her mind blank with confusion. Her chest heaved. Could it be as Reade had said? Had a procurer taken Sally?

Fighting tears, she stood unable to think as pedestrians pushed past her. Some glanced at her curiously, but no one stopped to ask if they could help. Jo waited. A sharp wind blew dark clouds overhead. Rain sent people scurrying. Water dripped off the brim of her hat, her parcels in danger of slipping from her shaky hands. Was she panicking unnecessarily? She tried to think. Sally must have dashed into a shop for something she'd seen and become lost. The maid would find her way back to Upper Brook Street. She seemed a capable, sensible girl.

When a hackney stopped for her, she climbed inside, damp and shivering.

Arriving home, she paid him and ran up the path, her arms full of parcels. The butler answered the knocker. "Mr. Spears," she gasped, gazing into eyes, which bore a distant expression. "Has my maid, Sally, arrived home?"

"I couldn't say, Miss Dalrymple. Servants do not enter through the front door if they know what is good for them."

With a frown, Jo dumped the packages and boxes at his feet and flew upstairs, and finding no sign of Sally, ran down to the servants' quarters. Two servants sat on the sofa in the servants' hall, resting between chores.

"Sally is not here, Miss Dalrymple," Agnes said.

"I haven't set eyes on Sally since she left with you this morning," the housekeeper confirmed, looking surprised. "Not like that girl to wander off. She has a good head on her shoulders."

That was what Jo thought, and it only frightened her. She climbed the stairs, weeping. Her father sat with Aunt Mary in the parlor. Between choking sobs and hiccoughs, Jo explained what had happened.

"My goodness, my girl, there's no need for this," he said soothingly, patting her on the back. "She has merely gone off on an errand of her own. You didn't see where she went?"

"No," Jo wailed. "Sally waited on the pavement with the packages while I went out onto the road to hail a hackney. One jarvey refused to stop," she confessed as her father's eyebrows lowered. "I stopped the next by waving my handkerchief."

"Sally will know the way home, Jo." Aunt Mary said. "She is more familiar with London streets than we are."

"Yes, that's true." Jo grasped it eagerly, desperate to believe it.

But the hours passed, and Sally did not come home.

They dispatched a servant to search the area where Sally disappeared. He returned two hours later with the distressing news that no one had seen a young blonde maid.

Jo's dinner sat untouched before her. As soon as she could, she went to her bedchamber and sat on the window seat watching the street. Her aunt brought a cup of hot chocolate and a plate of biscuits. She sat with Jo until she drank the whole cup and nibbled a biscuit and then urged her to get into bed. There was nothing she could do until morning, and Sally may well be home by then.

Heavy with exhaustion, Jo slid beneath the covers, but her mind was too busy for sleep. She kept returning to when Sally disappeared. There had been a lot of traffic on the road, she remembered. She barely took notice of the carriages which passed her, so intent was she in gaining the jarvey's attention. Surely someone would have seen something? She would return in the morning and make more inquiries, although in her heart she knew it was useless. Sally was not there. Where was she now? In danger? In pain? Or…worse? Her throat tight, Jo turned her face to the pillow and wept.

She had finally dropped off to sleep. When she woke, it seemed as if a lead weight had attached itself to her spine. She dressed quickly and ran up to the attics to the room Sally shared with Agnes, but Sally had not slept in her bed.

Jo went straight to the servants' hall, hoping she might have just arrived. She had not. No one had seen her. All the servants talked about it. The scullery maid suggested Sally had gone home to the country. "Some girls don't like it 'ere," she said. "Sally seemed happy here, though. Oh, I hope she's all right."

"London can be dangerous for the unwary," the housekeeper, Mrs. Cross, said grimly. "I advise all my maids to be careful. A girl can get in trouble in the blink of an eye."

A servant went out again to search the area. He came back and shook his head.

By luncheon, Jo was frantic. She roamed the dining room, unable to sit and eat. Who could she turn to for help? They must call a constable, but would he be able to help her, when Sally vanished yesterday? One name came into her mind. *Reade.* She hadn't forgiven him for interrogating her. But she still trusted Reade to accomplish what others could not.

A maid set plates of chicken soup before them. "I must speak to Lord Reade," Jo said, "The baron will help us." He might disapprove of her, but that hardly mattered if he found Sally.

"Why do you think that gentleman can help, Jo?" Aunt Mary asked. "You've only danced with him once, and a few days ago, you said you found him annoying."

"And we don't have his address," her father added, picking up his spoon.

"No, but the Cartwrights live in Grosvenor Square, which isn't far from here. We pass the square every day."

"Very well. I shan't risk this interfering with my digestion." Her father put down his napkin and, with a regretful glance at the soup, rose from the table. "I shall send a note to the Cartwrights."

"No! We must go to see them, Papa," Jo said. "They may not get the note for hours!"

"One doesn't just visit people unannounced, Jo," he said with a perplexed frown. "The Cartwrights are decent people, so I suppose they won't mind. But I'm not sure how they can help find your maid, do you?"

"Mr. Cartwright is sure to know where Lord Reade lives."

"And supposing he tells us? Although he may not wish to. One doesn't hand out addresses willy-nilly. The baron may be busy or away from London. And perhaps he won't care to find your maid." He patted her cheek. "I'm not sure what has happened to your usually sound reasoning. But I shall indulge you. The worst that can happen to us is we won't be permitted entry."

In the hall, her father shrugged into his coat. "Just don't get your hopes up, Jo."

"We must find her, Papa. I am responsible. And there's nothing else I can think to do." Jo tied the strings of her bonnet. "Mr. Spears, should Sally return before us, please tell her to await me in my bedchamber," she said to the butler.

"I shall instruct Mrs. Cross," Spears said, looking affronted.

The door knocker banged, echoing around the hall. Startled, they gazed at each other and waited in breathless anticipation as the butler stalked over to open it.

Sally huddled on the porch hatless, her eyes enormous pools of dark distress. Her rumpled skirts and pelisse looked damp and badly soiled, and her hair escaped down her neck.

"Sally!" Jo leaped forward and dragged the girl inside.

Sally shuddered. "I'm sorry, Miss Jo. I should go to the servant's entrance, but I've been so frightened."

With a sob of relief, Jo threw her arms around her. She drew the distressed girl into the parlor.

Her father shut the parlor door on the butler and went to the sideboard, where he removed the stopper from the sherry decanter.

Sally sank down on the sofa and struggled to get the words out while Jo fired off questions, the maid struggled to answer.

Her father handed Sally a glass of sherry. She took a long sip and coughed.

Jo, losing patience, took hold of her arm, almost spilling the drink. "What happened to you, Sally? Tell us quickly! We've been so worried!"

Her shoulders shook. "They kidnapped me." Tears tracked down her face.

"Kidnapped?" Reade had been right in warning her. Why hadn't she listened to him? Jo rummaged in her reticule and pressed the handkerchief into Sally's hand. "Did they hurt you? Who could have done such a dreadful thing?"

"They didn't hurt me, but I've no idea who they were," Sally wailed. "The strings on one parcel had come undone, and as I stooped down to retie it, a man grabbed me from behind. He put his hand over my mouth and bundled me into a carriage pulled up beside us. Before I could twist around to see who he was, he dragged a black hood over my head and shoved me to the floor. I tried to scream, but he poked me in the back and snarled at me. Told me to keep quiet, or he'd throttle me. I must have fainted because I remember very little of the journey or where we went."

"But I was only a little way down the street, hailing the hackney," Jo said. "Why did I not see?"

Sally took another sip of the drink and grimaced. "It happened so fast."

As she struggled with feelings of guilt, Jo stared at her aghast. "How did you escape?"

"I didn't." Sally gazed at her owlishly. "They took me somewhere. A noisy place. There was loud laughter. They pushed me into a room with my hands tied. I heard the door shut. My legs gave way, and I fell onto a dusty carpet and huddled there for hours. I must have fallen asleep. When I woke, I was ever so stiff. My arms hurt something awful with my hands tied behind my back. It must have been morning, although no light came through the hood. And I was devilishly hungry."

Sally drained the rest of the sherry and collapsed back against the sofa. "Then the door opened, and a woman came in. I smelled her strong lavender perfume. The woman must have stood looking at me for several minutes without speaking. I pleaded with her to let me go, but she went out and closed the door. I could hear them outside the room. She was arguing with the man. Fair yelling at him, she was. Ordered him to let me go straight away. He didn't want to, and I was almost sick with fear that he might persuade her to let him keep me.

But he finally agreed. I sagged with relief and could barely find my feet as he dragged me out into the air, the hood still over my head. It must have rained. I'd lost my hat, and the leaves dripped chilly water down my neck as he shoved me into a carriage."

Aunt Mary tutted. "You poor girl. What a dreadful experience."

"You are safe now," Jo's father said soothingly.

An inquisitive kitchen maid brought in the tea. Jo dismissed her and poured out cups, while Aunt Mary patted Sally's hand.

Jo stirred in lots of sugar and placed a cup before Sally. "How did you get home?"

"The carriage stopped not long after. He untied my hands and lifted me down onto the ground. It was cold but had stopped raining. He smelled clean, like a gentleman, and he had a starched cravat. I know starch. Used to do the laundry. Spoke proper, he did, but frosty, and fair chilled me through. Asked if I could count. I thought he was mad, but I said I had some learning from the parish school back home. Then he told me not to remove the blindfold until I'd counted to fifty. He sounded so menacing. I did what I was told. Must have counted to a hundred. I was never good at sums and feared I'd got it wrong.

"When I finally got up enough courage to remove the hood, I didn't know where I was. The street was strange to me. There were trees and gardens. And no traffic, and anyway, I had no money for a hackney. While I wondered what to do, a lady came out of a house across the street. Nicely dressed, she was. She asked me if she could help. When I explained what had happened, she was most sympathetic. Walked with me to the corner, although I still don't know where I was. A hackney came along, and she paid my fare."

"Oh, that was so good of her." Jo wondered why the lady hadn't called a constable.

"Yes, she was. Ever so kind."

Jo put her arm around the girl's trembling body. "Well, you're home now and safe."

"Yes. I shan't want to go out again," Sally said.

"You shall have a hearty dinner, a nice hot bath, and go to bed," Jo said with conviction.

"A hot bath?" Sally's eyes widened. "I should like that, Miss Jo."

"I'll send for a constable," Jo's father said. "We must report this incident. People cannot go about abducting maids."

Aunt Mary agreed.

Jo nodded but doubted anything would come of it. Poor Sally had nothing helpful to tell him. "When he lifted you down, did you sense anything else about him?"

"The man wasn't that strong because he struggled, even though I'm not heavy. He must have put his face near mine." She shivered. "I smelled licorice on his breath."

Jo nodded, disappointed. He liked sweets, which was no help to them at all. She glanced at her father and found him frowning thoughtfully.

"Papa?"

He shook his head and rose from his chair. "See to your maid," he said and left the room. "I need to speak to the butler."

Jo stared after him. What would he want with Spears? He could barely tolerate him.

The next day, Jo questioned Sally again. After a good night's sleep, the girl was in better spirits. "You said when he put you down, you'd only been traveling a short while."

"Yes."

"Can you remember anything you heard during that time?"

Sally thought for a while and then nodded. "We passed a crowd somewhere. I'm sorry. I was so frightened, and I could only think of him."

"Do you think you could find the street where the lady lived again?"

"I don't think I could," she said glumly. "I saw a sign pointing to

Soho Square, but that might not be of help."

"It must have cost a bit to take you to Mayfair," Jo said thoughtful-ly.

Sally nodded. "The woman asked him how much. She haggled a bit." She shivered. "I was afraid he might put me down somewhere on the way, but he brought me right to the door as she instructed."

"How very good of her," she said.

"Wasn't it? Most wouldn't give a toss or not have the money to spare," Sally said. "I don't think she was poor. I wanted to repay her somehow, but she refused."

The constable couldn't help them. Jo considered taking Sally in a hackney back the way they'd come, with the chance that something might jog her memory. But she decided against it because it might be too distressing for Sally, who seemed to have blotted out the frighten-ing experience.

FINALLY, FREE OF commitments, Reade checked on those shadowing the Virdens two days later. It was early morning when he approached a colleague stationed in an overgrown garden near the Virden's house. "They gave Johns the slip yesterday, sir." Reade's most reliable man, Winston Black, came up to him with a nod of welcome. "Left their carriage standing outside the front entrance and went out through the rear of the property. Not sure what form of transport they used. Asked the jarvies in the area. Nothing."

"Bloody hell." Through the trees, Reade's gaze settled on the house across the lane. No sign of the Virdens. A moment later, some curtains opened. A maid came out the back door and banged a broom against a wall.

"Think they've cottoned on that they're being watched?"

"Don't know, sir," Black said. "Might just be cautious."

"If they have, it will make things difficult. What happened during the night?"

"He attended a ball. She didn't go out. Lord Rivenstock came home with Virden in the early hours. He didn't stay long. I couldn't hear what they spoke of, but it was the devil of an argument. He left, glowering, and muttering about something."

Reade crossed his arms and leaned against a tree. "Get some sleep. I'll stay until Johns arrives. Let's hope he can keep his wits about him this time."

"Yes, sir." Black shuffled wearily away.

Reade remained where he had an unrestricted view of the house. It drizzled. He cursed and turned up the collar of his greatcoat as water dripped off his hat. The Virdens might still be abed.

A window on the ground floor opened. The breakfast room. Bent low, Reade crossed the lane and vaulted a fence. He flattened himself against the wall outside the breakfast room.

The clink of cutlery and rattle of crockery greeted him through the open window, and the rich aroma of coffee and buttered toast floated out. Reade tried to ignore the rumble of his stomach, reminding him he had yet to eat breakfast.

"There's no appeasing Rivenstock," Virden said. "Since you made me break my promise of that plump partridge for him."

"Pah! What were you thinking?" she snarled. "It could have ruined your chances with the girl! We shall have to act quickly to placate him. And as it is your fault, I expect you to resolve it."

"I intend to very shortly." Virden's words sounded muffled, his mouth full of sausage, probably. Reade recognized the savory aroma. "I have a ripe pigeon ready for the plucking."

"Better be a good one," she snapped. "Not a turkey like the last one. Be sure they fit our requirements," she said. "No slipups or our overseas customers will turn nasty. You can't trust these foreigners."

"I'll take it in hand," he said and chuckled.

"None of that. We must deliver our goods in the condition we found them, understand?"

"Yes," he said, sounding resentful.

"And then turn your attention to that other matter. This tomfoolery has kept you from the plan we have for a certain young lady."

"I don't know why you want me to go to all that trouble," he grumbled.

"Because he'll pay up big, that's why. I have it on good authority that his pockets are deep."

"Weren't you going to entice him to the altar? You could have his money all to yourself. Legitimately, too."

"He'd drag me off to some backwater. I'd have to kill him to escape. He'd take years to marry me, anyway. He's still in love with his dead wife."

"Better than me having to pretend a passion I don't feel. At least at your age…"

A cup crashed into its saucer. She snarled, "You'd like that, wouldn't you? You could retire on my money, put your feet up, that's your style, isn't it?"

"I'll make my own."

She sighed. "But you always think small. That's the trouble with you. Now your stepfather, Virden, he thought big, he did."

"Didn't do him much good, did it? Common muck he was."

"You're always going on about class! We have partners to consider. Not men I fancy crossing. They'd cut your throat soon as look at you." A chair scraped back.

Reade decided he'd pushed his luck long enough and returned the way he came.

When Johns arrived full of apologies for having slipped up, Reade left him and went in search of a hackney to take him to the inn he favored. He must then visit Whitehall to discuss the ins and outs of

Rivenstock's visit and the interesting conversation he'd just overheard. It was regrettable that they'd mentioned no names except for Rivenstock. But he was still confident they would. He'd have these two and Rivenstock watched around the clock.

It was only a matter of time before they made a wrong move. They sounded too confident, taking risks. They'd got away with it this time, but they wouldn't again. When criminals believed they were invincible, that's when it all fell to pieces.

CHAPTER TEN

A T THE NEXT ball, Charlotte Graham came to sit with Jo. They watched the passing parade of renowned guests as Charlotte identified each by name. "That's Sir Lumley St. George Skeffington, Baronet," she murmured about a short, thin man with rouged cheeks dressed in elaborate dandy's clothes. "And that's the very fashionable Duke of Rutland with his wife, Elizabeth. They are talking to Viscount Petersham. Isn't he handsome?"

"He is," Jo dutifully responded, gazing at the gentleman with the small, pointed beard.

"Petersham is Lord of the Bedchamber to the king and is close to the Prince Regent."

Charlotte turned to Jo with an infectious grin. "Mr. Gerald Virden came to tea yesterday. He has excellent manners. He brought my chaperone a posy of flowers from Covent Garden. Mrs. Lincoln is very pleased. She is hopeful he will offer for me."

Virden. That was the name Reade had questioned Jo about in the garden. "I haven't met Mr. Virden," she said. "Can you point him out?"

Charlotte scanned the ballroom. "He rarely dances. We spoke earlier tonight in one of the reception rooms. He inquired after my chaperone's health." Her eyes sparkled. "He's such a thoughtful gentleman. Mrs. Lincoln is unwell. When he invited me for a drive in his curricle to Hyde Park, she worried that she couldn't accompany us. He was at pains to reassure her it was permissible for an unengaged couple to ride alone in an open carriage."

"Yes, Mrs. Millet, who is very knowledgeable about such things, has said the same thing."

Might Reade be here tonight? Would he wish to speak to Mr. Virden? He'd been so overbearing, questioning her at the rout. She didn't see why she should be so obliging as to tell him.

"I can't see him," Charlotte confirmed after making a careful study of the guests. "He must have left. But I shall see him tomorrow. Mrs. Lincoln is most impressed with him."

Jo frowned. Why was Reade so interested in this man? And why did he think her father knew him? "What is Mr. Virden like?"

"He is of moderate height. You would notice him. He is handsome, and his smile makes my heart beat faster." Charlotte giggled and patted Jo's arm. "I feel I can say anything to you, Jo. I am pleased we're friends. Since Anabel Riley left London, I've been lonely. Some of the debs are uppish, and some are just plain silly. Will you attend the Brandworth's Venetian breakfast?"

"Yes, we are going."

"I will tell you all about my outing in the park with Mr. Virden when we meet again."

"Yes, please do. I am eager to hear all about it."

As the musicians returned to the dais, Charlotte rose. "A waltz is about to be called. I won't dance, but I must return to Mrs. Lincoln. It was so sweet of her to come tonight when I am sure she would prefer her bed."

Charlotte hurried away as couples gathered on the dance floor. Reade appeared, outpacing another gentleman with the same intention. He offered her his hand and smiled down at her. Jo felt a sense of warm recognition. As if he was an old friend. How silly of her when he had been so maddening when they last met. Why did he wish to see her? To grill her further about Virden?

His hand settled low on her back, and she struggled to remember what it was she wished to tell him. Just being near him made her brain turn to mush. "Mr. Virden was here tonight," she said as he swept her into the dance.

He cast her an ironic look. "I didn't think you knew the fellow."

"I don't." His hard stare ruffled her. "But my friend, Charlotte, does. She saw him earlier this evening."

"Here, was he? And you didn't see him?"

"No, I wasn't with her. You aren't about to interrogate me again, are you? I thought we'd finished with that."

A smile teased his lips. "No, I will not *interrogate* you. And no, we are not finished."

"Well." Jo huffed. "How annoying you are."

He laughed.

"Is there a purpose to this dance?"

"A purpose? You are refreshingly different, Miss Dalrymple. Ladies usually flirt with gentlemen when they dance."

Ladies would flirt with him, she thought, catching her bottom lip in her teeth. But she was just as hopeless. She loved being in his arms, even though what passed between them was too serious for frivolity. She suspected there was always a purpose behind Reade's actions. And she intended to find out what it was.

The glorious music swelled as they glided over the floor. Jo closed her eyes for a moment. When she opened them, Reade's dark brown eyes had softened. "You enjoy this piece?"

"Yes, very much." It wasn't the music, it was being close to him. It emboldened her to flirt a little. "I know if I close my eyes, you will keep me safe."

Her attempt at flirtation failed, for his gaze sharpened. "On a dance floor. But keeping you safe outside of a ballroom might be harder."

She almost gasped at the change in him. "Am I at risk of harm?"

"You, and every young woman in London."

This was more than an idle warning. What did he refer to? She must tell him about Sally. Impossible while waltzing with him. Jo fell silent as the dance continued. Reade didn't question her lack of conversation. He seemed absorbed in his own thoughts.

The dance ended.

They crossed the floor toward where Aunt Mary sat with her friend, Mrs. Butterworth. Jo's father was talking to some people farther down the room. Who knew when she would see Reade again. She steeled herself. "My maid, Sally, was abducted from Piccadilly while we were shopping," she said. "And before you scold me for venturing out without a proper escort, I must explain that Sally arrived home unscathed the following day."

His hand tightened over hers, halting her. "They snatched her from the street? Was she molested?"

"No, not that. The most extraordinary thing. A man put a hood over her head and took her to a house and then…"

"Not here." Reade took her by the elbow and led her out through the French doors. On the terrace, a cool breeze swept across her hot face. Jo noted his grim expression in consternation. Why had she told him? He was angry with her, although what right he had to be so was beyond her. It had been so frightening to lose Sally that she did feel guilty, and waited, tensing for the rebuke.

"Tell me the whole." The concern in his dark eyes made Jo's chest tighten and fight tears. It was not what she'd expected. She related the incident while he prodded her for more information. "I don't know where he took Sally, but the hackney bringing her home passed a sign to Soho Square." She glanced anxiously up into his face. Reade's heavy eyebrows lowered, his expression dark and angry. She quaked, for his reaction frightened her. "Sally *has* fully recovered."

"I am sorry your maid has suffered such an ordeal." His quiet voice surprised her. "Sally is a fortunate young woman."

"Fortunate?" Ice trickled down Jo's spine. She shivered. "Is she safe now?"

"Yes, it appears they don't want her." He moved close, and she drew in an anxious breath, finding his masculine smell reassuring. "Joanna," he murmured, his use of her first name startling her. "You must be very careful." His eyes were steely and yet imploring. "Promise me?"

Jo swallowed. "Yes. I wish you'd tell me why they took Sally. You know, don't you?"

"I am fairly sure someone intended Sally for a brothel. And something made them change their mind."

Her throat had become tight, and she struggled to speak. "But what could it be, Reade?"

"I don't know, but I don't like it." He turned away from her and rested his hands on the banister rail, staring out into the dark gardens. "I intend to find out. If anything happens which worries you, send word to me at my rooms at Albany in Piccadilly."

Jo shivered. Did he expect something bad to happen?

His long fingers curled around hers and gently squeezed. "I've frightened you," he said, his voice low. "You can come to me." He paused. "Not at Albany. Your presence at a gentleman's residence would not go unnoticed. We must arrange a suitable meeting place."

"But...where?" she drew out, still trembling.

"Do you ride?"

"Yes. I hadn't planned to in London. There's no reason why I can't hire a couple of hacks at the Hyde Park stables for Sally and me."

"If you need my advice, or if something important occurs, send me a feather."

She stared at him. "A feather?"

"I'm sure your hats can spare one. Best we meet before the fashionable hour. Let's make it noon at the Brook Street gate."

"Yes. Thank you, that has put my mind at rest."

"And should you encounter Virden, or see him with your father, I want to hear about it."

"My father doesn't know…"

"We shall see." He cut her off and took her arm. They returned to the ballroom. Her father was in his chair.

After Reade bowed and left them, her father frowned after him. "What were you doing on the terrace with the baron?"

Jo sank onto the chair, wrung out. "Just taking the air, Papa."

"I don't like it. That fellow worries me. He's an unscrupulous rake, Jo."

"No, he is not." While she'd seen Reade flirt with other women, he seemed disinclined to do it with her. It was better he didn't. He would make a terrible husband. She wondered why her father had such a poor opinion of him.

Jo debated whether to tell her father what she and Reade had discussed. She decided against it. It would only worry him when it wasn't likely anything untoward would happen. And if she had to meet Reade in the park, her father would never allow it. Riding with him would be so wonderful, she almost hoped something would happen. How foolish she was about Reade. She heaved a sigh and searched the guests for Mr. Ollerton. She'd expected him to be here tonight. It appeared his interest in her had cooled. The possibility failed to disappoint her.

AT WHITEHALL, THE next day, Reade discussed the matter with Cartwright.

"It makes sense," Cartwright said. "They abandoned the maid because people would make a fuss and hunt for her. Strange, though, that it was the Dalrymple's maid."

"That's what worries me," Reade said heavily.

"What do you think of Dalrymple? Might he be involved in this business?"

"I very much doubt it, although Virden might have wanted something from him. Running one of his scams, perhaps. We'll keep an eye on him and step in if we must."

Cartwright looked surprised. "You haven't questioned him? Is it because of his daughter?"

Reade scowled. "It's better not to alert him and possibly Virden that he's under observation. I'm surprised you'd think I'd allow an attachment to a lady to affect my judgment."

"No need to growl at me like a bear. You wouldn't be the first man," Cartwright said with a subtle wink.

Reade grinned. "I have had a degree of difficulty, I might add." He pushed away the image of a soft, wide mouth, perfect for kissing. He'd been a whisker from doing precisely that in the Feldman's garden. "But I have no intention of pursuing Miss Dalrymple."

"While I admit to disappointment that you won't court the pretty lady, I understand your reluctance," Cartwright said. "We men cling to our freedom, and then once given up, we wonder why it took us so long."

Reade cocked an eyebrow. "I realize that as a married man, you consider it your duty to persuade your bachelor friends to embrace the parson's mousetrap." Reade gave the hint of a smile. "But I don't intend to marry for a while. I beg you to warn me should I appear to be in any danger of it."

Cartwright nodded, a spark of humor in his eyes. "You can rely on me."

"Brandon, I can rely on you to watch my back should we be facing a gang of footpads in an alley, but I don't feel so confident in London ballrooms."

Cartwright chuckled. "That would depend on the circumstances."

Reade threw up his hands and laughed. "Going into politics soon?"

CHAPTER ELEVEN

C HARLOTTE FAILED TO appear at the Venetian breakfast, which proved to be just that, a tasty breakfast served around midday, and neither did she come to the picnic in Richmond the following Thursday. Had Mrs. Lincoln's ill health kept Charlotte at home?

The next morning, Mr. Ollerton left his card. He called after three o'clock. Jo had just farewelled Mrs. Brownley and her daughter, Caroline, who'd issued an invitation to a musicale the following Saturday.

"I've come in the hope you'll allow me to drive you to the park tomorrow, Miss Dalrymple. They have mended my carriage at last," Mr. Ollerton said, taking a seat in the parlor.

How attractive was his smile? She'd forgotten. "I should be delighted." Jo was pleased to see him again. How at ease he was chatting with Aunt Mary. So very good-natured.

When he left, her aunt was full of praise for him. "Few gentleman have such exquisite manners," she said. "Do you think you might develop a tendre for him, Jo?"

Jo wanted to say yes, but a large dark-haired man whose heavy brows often drew together in a scowl rendered her silent. Was she falling in love with Reade?

"Your father worries that you might become too fond of Baron Reade," Aunt Mary said as if reading Jo's thoughts.

Jo gaped at her aunt. "Why? Did Papa give a reason?"

"Not precisely, but you have a certain way of looking at him."

"I don't think I look at Reade differently to any other gentleman." *Did she? Was she that obvious?*

"And the way he looks at you."

Jo's heart thumped. "What do you mean, Aunt?"

"I can't put it into words." Thankfully, Aunt Mary's eyes remained on her knitting. "But I recognize that look."

How could her maiden aunt know such things? A shiver of yearning passed through her. It was entirely too foolish to think of Reade that way. But she couldn't help it. Even though she reminded herself of the many reasons she shouldn't, she woke each day hoping to see him again. But while Reade wished to protect her from harm, he did not love her. And he had no intention of marrying.

She must give Mr. Ollerton a chance. "Mr. Ollerton wishes to take me for a drive to the park tomorrow." It was always difficult to distract her aunt once she'd settled on a course of conversation.

"How pleasant," Aunt Mary said, winding wool into a ball. "You make me wish I was young again, Jo."

She had often wondered about her aunt. "Was there never anyone you wished to marry?"

Aunt Mary's cheeks grew pink, and her eyes behind the lenses of her glasses became misty. "When I was young. Lord Denzil, Fallbrook's heir, and I were to become engaged after he returned from the war." She took up her needles again. "But he did not come back."

"Oh, Aunt, I'm sorry. I didn't know."

"He was the one. I wanted no one else."

The one. For some women, was there only one true love? And should fate intervene to break them apart, could another man's love ever be as sweet? Might Jo be one of those women? She feared she could be. As it was for her father. Although he had been seeing more of Mrs. Millet. He'd taken the lady to tea this afternoon. Jo had still failed to warm to Mrs. Millet. But she wanted her father to find happiness again. She picked up the ball of wool that rolled onto the floor and replaced it on the chair. "If Charlotte doesn't appear at the Johnson's card party tonight, I'll call on her tomorrow, before my carriage ride with Mr. Ollerton. She gave me Mrs. Lincoln's address."

"Quite the correct thing to do, Jo. I shall come with you. I'll take some chicken soup. Cook swears it's a cure for all ills."

Charlotte wasn't at the card party. Perhaps she hadn't received an invitation. Jo played several hands of whist but found it hard to concentrate. Reade did not come, nor did Mr. Ollerton, and the evening seemed overlong. When it drew to a close, she was pleased to go home.

After luncheon the next day, she and Aunt Mary called on Mrs. Lincoln.

Mrs. Lincoln, a small bird-like lady, rose from her chair when the maid admitted them. She clutched a handkerchief in her fingers. "Have you news of Charlotte?"

"No," Jo said with alarm. "She is not here?"

"No. Oh! I was hoping…" Mrs. Lincoln's eyes were red-rimmed, her white cap askew. "Do sit down, please, Miss Hatton, Miss Dalrymple."

She sent the maid away with the chicken soup. "When did you last see Charlotte, Miss Dalrymple? I am beside myself with worry. She went out days ago and did not come home."

Jo gasped. "Where did she go?"

"Mr. Verdin took Charlotte for a ride in his carriage to the park. A delightful gentleman. He called Charlotte yesterday in answer to my letter and expressed his surprise and dismay to learn she hadn't returned. He'd left Charlotte at the gate after she'd asked him not to accompany her to the door." Her eyes filled with tears. "But why would she do such a thing and not come inside? Have I been unfair to her? Has she returned to the country? I have heard nothing! What if she has eloped with a gentleman?" She reached for her smelling salts with a trembling hand. "I declare, I am close to hysterics! Her grandfather must be informed. I shall write today. I have delayed writing in the hope she would return."

"Shouldn't you call a constable?" Aunt Mary asked.

Mrs. Lincoln's face paled. "But that would cause a dreadful scandal. It would end any chance Charlotte might have for a good marriage. Her grandfather would blame me. He would say I have been lax in my duties." She looked up at them imploringly. "Have I been too careless? I believed it was proper for her to ride in the park in an open carriage with a gentleman. It was a curricle, so I could not have gone with them."

"It was perfectly acceptable," Jo said. "Might someone have seen her? Your neighbors?"

Mrs. Lincoln sagged in her seat. "I asked our neighbor, an elderly gentleman, but he never puts a toe out the door. The house on the other side is empty. I didn't consider it wise to knock on doors. Gossip spreads so quickly in London."

Jo leaned over and patted the lady's trembling hand. "I shall make discreet inquiries, Mrs. Lincoln. We will find Charlotte, never fear." But how very odd it was. Charlotte had not mentioned a gentleman apart from Mr. Virden. This didn't seem like her at all. She must ask Reade for help. She would send him a feather in the hope he would meet her in the park. Jo stood. "I must go, Mrs. Lincoln. Please send a note if you hear from Charlotte."

"You don't wish for tea?"

"No, thank you. I have something urgent I must do."

"That poor woman," Aunt Mary said in the hackney on the way home. "Do you think Charlotte has run away with some man?"

Jo frowned. "I find it hard to believe. It seems most unlike her."

"What are you going to do, Jo?"

"I will ask Lord Reade to help us. He has invited me to ride in the park with him," Jo said.

"But what about Mr. Ollerton?"

Jo took Aunt Mary's hand. "Aunt, I need you to do something for me you will not like. I don't have Mr. Ollerton's address, so when he comes to take me out, you must make my apologies. Will you tell him something urgent has come up? Say I had to rush away to help a friend."

"Oh, dear. I'm not good at this, Jo. I always thought, hoped, that you and he…"

Jo thought of Sally's experience and couldn't help fearing the worst. "Charlotte's life might depend upon us acting quickly."

"But what can you do to help? Your father won't approve of you riding with Lord Reade. You know he doesn't like him. And Mr. Ollerton will be quite put out. I shake at the thought of telling him. I am not good at deception."

"It isn't a lie, Aunt Mary. I am trying to help a friend." The hackney pulled up, and she helped her aunt down, then opened her coin purse to pay the jarvey.

She passed her aunt on the steps. "I shall have to hurry. I'm sorry, but I fear for poor Charlotte. London is a dangerous place. Remember what happened to Sally."

"My goodness," Aunt Mary murmured as she followed her inside.

Jo sent for Sally and ran upstairs to her bedchamber. When the maid came in, Jo was struggling with the buttons on her rifle-green habit. She went to the mirror and put on her wide-brimmed black hat. "Have you something suitable to wear horse riding, Sally?"

Sally gasped. "No, Miss Jo."

"You have ridden a horse?"

"Yes, old Peter, the farmer's horse."

"Then we must find you a good-natured mount," Jo said. "I brought my old riding habit with me, the gray wool, I think it will fit you." Jo plucked a feather from a bonnet. "Put it on while I go down to give this feather to Jed."

"Why would the footman need an ostrich feather, Miss Jo?"

"I haven't time to explain, Sally. Hurry and dress, please."

In the library, Jo tucked the feather within the folds of a letter, added Reade's address, and marked it urgent. She went in search of Jed and found him with the butler in the cellar. Aware of the sharp eye of Mr. Spears, she gave Jed careful instructions.

"Go now, please."

"Yes, Miss Dalrymple."

"And return immediately to complete your duties," Mr. Spears said. "Don't dawdle."

Jo hurried upstairs. What if Reade didn't get the letter today? She would ride every afternoon until he came. But she sensed time was crucial, although she did not understand why. It seemed absurd to imagine Charlotte snatched from outside her home in a respectable part of town. But where else might she have gone? Reade would listen and do what he could to find her. She had complete trust in him.

At the Hyde Park stables in Westbourne Street, Jo chose a hack for herself, a neat roan mare. They mounted Sally on a smaller bay with calm eyes.

They reined in inside the Brook Street gate. Jo glanced at the watch pinned to her chest. It was almost noon. "We shall have to wait, Sally."

Sally rode her horse up and down the strip of grass. "Is this to be another adventure, Miss Jo?"

"Not like the last one, thank the Lord," Jo said. "Shall we dismount?"

It was half-past twelve, and the horses were growing restive when Reade, in a black coat, buckskins, and glossy riding boots, rode through the gate on a beautiful steel gray horse. Jo's heart hammered as she fought to put into words what she must tell him. He did not look happy to see her.

He greeted them both as he pulled up. "Well, Miss Dalrymple, shall we trot the horses down Rotten Row?"

Jo turned her horse's head to follow him. Even at this unfashionable hour, a few riders cantered down the Row, and carriages circled on the South Carriage drive.

Jo was conscious only of Reade. "I'm so glad you came." It gave her a jolt to recognize how important he'd become in her life.

Reade angled Ash in beside her mount. "What has brought you here, Miss Dalrymple?"

"Something terribly worrying has happened," she gasped. With a deep breath, she rushed to tell him. "My friend Charlotte Graham has disappeared."

MISS DALRYMPLE, JOANNA, was clearly frightened. Reade glanced back at the young maid trailing behind them. "Tell me more slowly," he ordered, his voice low and insistent, his attention caught by a fiery lock curling against her satiny cheek and her firm little chin beneath the black hat. "Charlotte went to the park with Mr. Virden in his curricle. But he left her at the gate. Her chaperone hasn't seen her since."

His blood ran cold. "She was with Virden?"

"Yes, and I thought…"

"Thoughts have no place here," he said, concern making him abrupt. "We need to look at the facts. Did Miss Graham mention anything that might help us find her?"

Her scared eyes sought his. "I've been going over and over it. Only that Mr. Virden expressed an interest in her. She thought he might propose."

"What are her circumstances?"

"Charlotte lives with Mrs. Lincoln, the lady her grandfather engaged as her chaperone. Her grandfather lives in the country."

"Is the family affluent?"

"Not especially. Charlotte said she didn't have a large dowry. She has no other relatives." She swallowed the lump in her dry throat. "Something else I recalled, which may have no bearing on this, but Charlotte mentioned a debutante, Anabel Riley, who suddenly disappeared last Season."

He nodded. "We must deal first with Charlotte, but tell me about Anabel, and describe Charlotte to me."

"Anabel was an orphan, staying with an aged aunt who has since died. That's all I know about her. Charlotte is above average height and very slender. She has golden hair and brown eyes."

As they walked the horses, he listened while Joanna told him about the young lady. "She considers herself too tall to attract a husband, but her grandfather is determined to see her wed."

What had Virden done with her? Got one of his scoundrels to kidnap her? Would the girl stand a chance when she'd been gone for days? He doubted anything could be done for Anabel. Were either of them still in London? Or even alive? He ordered his thoughts for the search, which he would put in motion as soon as he left Joanna. They reined in at the end of the Row. "I'll ride with you to the stables."

Her eyes beseeched him. "Reade, what will you do to find her?"

"I intend to look for her, Joanna. But you must leave it in my hands."

"Do you think a procuress abducted Anabel and Charlotte?"

He cursed under his breath. Joanna was smart. He might have known she'd consider the possibility. He didn't want her anywhere near this investigation. "There are many reasons for a girl to leave London. Not all of them bad."

"I know you will find her, but let me help, please. Tell me what to do."

It tore at him to see the trust in her eyes. She believed he wrought miracles. He could not tell her of his worst fears. "You will help me by staying safe and letting me deal with it."

"Do you think the same people took Charlotte as those who abducted Sally?"

"That I don't know. If I have news, I'll send you a note. In the meantime, I'll advise Bow Street."

"I thought we might utilize Sally's experience to find her."

He groaned inwardly. "I don't see how."

She looked at him keenly. "We could retrace the route the jarvey took when he drove Sally home." Jo glanced behind her. A group of riders had captured Sally's attention. "Sally might remember something which leads us to the lady who helped her. Anything might happen after that. But I wish I knew why they let Sally go."

His jaw tightened. "Most probably because she has people who care about her."

"But Charlotte has Mrs. Lincoln."

"We don't know yet what happened to Charlotte. London is a big city." His gaze took in the determined set of her slim shoulders and her curvy figure in the riding clothes. "But I promise you, I'll do my utmost to find her, even if she has married and is living in Scotland." Was it a reckless promise?

"If she planned to marry, Charlotte would have confided in Mrs. Lincoln. I believe she was fond of her and would not want her to worry. She would also have told me." She paused. "You think something terrible has happened to her, don't you?"

"Let's wait, shall we, until we find out more."

"I know you will do all you can, Reade."

They joined Sally and turned the horses toward the park stables.

"I wonder if Mr. Ollerton might be an acquaintance of yours?" she asked. "He recently called on us."

He frowned. There seemed a lot of gentlemen calling on Joanna. "Ollerton? I don't believe so. Who is he?"

"The second son of Viscount Cranswick."

What the devil? Reade turned to her sharply. "I'll escort you home."

"There is no need. Sally is with me, and it's only a few blocks from the stables to my home."

"Indulge me. You have exhibited a knack for getting yourself into hostile situations."

"In Mayfair?" She turned on the saddle to scowl at him. "That hardly seems fair."

"I know of Viscount Cranswick. He hails from the north, as do I. To my knowledge, he has only one son."

"But can you be sure of that?" she asked as they rode across the grass.

"Do not see him again."

"You are ordering me?" She raised delicate eyebrows. "Aren't you being a trifle hasty? You said you don't know him."

"It's not an order," he said evenly, aware that commanding Joanna to do anything was unwise. "I am appealing to your commonsense. That fellow is obviously not who he says he is."

"But he described his father and his home so vividly! Even his brother, Julian, who is away in the navy. Do you suspect Mr. Ollerton to be a fortune hunter? I believe you are mistaken. He has expressed a desire for a quiet life in the country and is about to purchase a small property with money inherited from his mother. He is very polite. Aunt Mary is most impressed with him."

"Then it appears he is a consummate liar." Reade gripped the reins. Had she succumbed to a scoundrel's charm? Damn it. He disliked being taken by surprise, and this was an unexpected and alarming occurrence.

"You accuse him of deceit. Yet you don't know him."

Reade clamped his lips on a curse. "We have your friend to concern us, until then, will you heed my advice?"

"But Mr. Ollerton will wonder at the change in me. He was to drive me to the park today, but I had to refuse him so I might meet you."

He tightened his jaw. "It can't be helped."

"Yes, I quite see that. I just want to find Charlotte safe and well."

Had he convinced Jo? She must obey him. If anything happened to her... He wrestled with unsettling emotions as he assisted the two women down from the horses.

They left the stables, and leading Ash by the reins, he walked with them up the road. Reade had wanted an uncomplicated life devoid of emotion, but he'd begun to wonder if that were true. His feelings deepened every time he saw Joanna. He couldn't deal with it now. Emotions had no place here.

"Will you promise me not to go anywhere with Ollerton?" Outside her home, Reade mounted Ash and gazed down at her, noting the distress in her eyes and the determined shape of her mouth.

"I have no interest in seeing Mr. Ollerton. It's Charlotte I care about. Please send word the minute you hear anything."

With a bob, Sally disappeared down the steps to the servants' quarters.

Charlotte had fallen foul of Virden. They had him under surveillance, so Black would know if the scoundrel left her safely outside her chaperone's house. If Virden had whisked the girl away, they would know where he took her. But something was amiss. Reade would have received word about it by now.

He hadn't been about to risk revealing any of this to Joanna. She was so concerned for her friend he wasn't confident she would leave the matter in his hands and go off tracing the maid's journey, which might lead her into danger. The thought of losing her sent a bolt of fear through him. It pulled him up short. She was coming to mean too much to him.

CHAPTER TWELVE

R EADE'S EYES SEARCHED hers. "Joanna, promise me you won't take any risks. I want nothing to happen to you."

Her name on his lips made Jo weak at the knees. She wanted to run into his arms and have him carry her away. She wasn't practical Jo from the country who knew what she wanted from life. Oh, God, she wanted him. His voice was low, husky, and imploring. Her pulse thrummed. She searched his eyes, which could look like brown velvet or hard as granite, depending on his mood. Was it concern or something more he felt for her? Or would she spend her life comparing every other man she met unfavorably to him?

His dark eyebrows lowered. "Promise?" he asked again, leaning forward in the saddle.

"I promise. Just find her, Reade," she repeated. It wasn't a lie. She wouldn't be reckless.

"Shall I send you another feather if I hear anything more?" she called after him.

He shook his head, but a reluctant smile teased his lips. "A note will suffice. I pray there is no necessity for it."

He urged his horse into a trot and left her.

A little giddy, she turned and climbed the steps. The parlor curtain twitched. With a sigh, she entered through the door held open by the butler.

"Mr. Ollerton has called, Miss Dalrymple," Spears announced in a disapproving tone.

Alarm, like a cool breeze, crept up the back of her neck and brought her down with a thud. "Did my aunt speak to him, Spears?"

"He is with your aunt. They are in the parlor."

Jo straightened her shoulders and entered the parlor.

Ollerton rose to his feet from beside her aunt on the sofa, where he appeared very much at home.

"Mr. Ollerton. How opportune to find you here, I planned to send you a note of apology."

"Ah, Miss Dalrymple."

Aunt Mary smiled up at her. "Jo, dear, I was just telling Mr. Ollerton how sorry you would be to miss him."

Mr. Ollerton bowed. "I was most disappointed, Miss Dalrymple, but here you are."

"I must apologize. It was a matter of some urgency, Mr. Ollerton," Jo said, seating herself opposite him in an armchair. Before she could dredge up a convincing explanation, he held up his hand to silence her. "No need to apologize. Miss Hatton has told me about your missing friend, Miss Graham. It is most concerning. Have you learned anything about her whereabouts?"

"No, I'm afraid not." Jo took the cup and saucer from Aunt Mary. "There seems nothing we can do. Charlotte might have left London."

He raised his fair eyebrows. "Indeed? With no word to Mrs. Lincoln? While I hate to be condemning, it is not how a person should behave."

"I'm sure Charlotte had good reason. I shall not judge her."

"Quite so. How generous." His smile seemed brittle and insincere to her, or was it because of Reade's warning? Could Ollerton be one of those fortune hunters they spoke of? "You must forgive me. I am a trifle out of sorts. They have discovered another problem with my carriage. A crack in the axle. Your poor opinion of me for breaking our engagement distressed me so much, I had to come and explain."

"That was good of you." Without putting it into words, he pointed out how remiss she'd been not to notify him. She considered it manipulation and refused to apologize to him again.

He rose to make his departure and spent several minutes fawning, in Jo's opinion, over Aunt Mary. Jo went out with him to find Sally hovering in the hall.

Mr. Ollerton moved past her maid without a glance.

"I need to see you in my bedchamber, Sally," Jo said.

At the door, Ollerton would not take no for an answer as he extracted a promise to ride to the park with him when his carriage was, at last, in working order.

Jo returned to her aunt. Was he the fraud Reade had suggested? It was possible, although it no longer mattered. She would not see Ollerton again. Reade, whether there was ever anything more between them, filled her head, her heart, and her dreams.

"Such a pleasant gentleman." Aunt Mary had taken up her knitting. "I hope you approve of me telling him about Miss Graham. When he stood before me looking so dreadfully disappointed, I quaked and found I had nothing in my head! And then the idea came to me. For one should always stick as close to the truth as one can, my father always said."

"That was wise, Aunt. Where is Papa?"

"Mrs. Millet invited him to view the silverware gallery at the museum, as your father has an interest in engraved pieces." Aunt Mary's needles flew, the gloves she knitted taking shape. "I believe he grows fond of the lady, Jo."

"It has occurred to me, too," Jo admitted.

"I should be happy for him," her aunt said. "But I cannot like it."

Jo had been caught up with thoughts of Reade. Her aunt's words brought her back with a jolt. "You dislike Mrs. Millet?"

"I can't imagine her living in Marlborough. She seems very much at home here in London." Aunt Mary looked up, concerned. "She told me about her cozy cottage here and how she loves her garden, especially her potted camellias. They are in flower. As the plant rarely does well in the city, she considers it quite an achievement. I just can't imagine your father being content living in London, can you?"

"No. He misses our home, his friends, and Sooty." Jo sipped the tea. She found it difficult to place her father with Mrs. Millet here, or anywhere. But he may marry whomever he chose. She trusted he would be happy for her to do the same. "I must ask Papa why he doesn't like Lord Reade," she said, biting into a jam tartlet.

"It was something Mrs. Millet said to him."

Jo frowned. "What was that?"

"Mrs. Millet said the baron was a heartless rake who left a young woman…" she flushed and ducked her head, "at the altar when she was expecting his child!"

"What nonsense! I don't believe it," Jo said promptly.

"Oh, Jo, do be careful. He could be a despicable rake."

"He isn't, Aunt Mary. I am not easily taken in."

Jo would know instinctively if it were true. She could never be drawn to such a man. But why would Mrs. Millet say such a thing? Letty had warned Jo against Reade, but that was because he didn't plan to marry. Letty would not be on such friendly terms with him if he'd behaved so immorally. And if Mrs. Millet had heard such awful gossip, then Letty would have, too.

Jo made her way up the stairs to her bedchamber. She sought peace to think about Reade. What he had told her, but also how grave he'd looked. Her musings went on to his graceful stride and the way he moved his dark head, his deep voice. His strength and the masterful way he handled the big horse. A thrill went through her as she recalled being held in his muscular arms. But even in her dreams, she could not forget that he was merely intent on keeping her safe from harm.

When Jo entered her bedchamber, Sally stood nervously, coiling her hands in her apron.

"Has something upset you, Sally?"

"It was that gentleman, Miss Jo."

"Mr. Ollerton?"

Sally nodded, her eyes owlish. "I smelled it again."

Jo frowned. "You seem upset. Come and sit down."

Sally perched on the edge of a chair, her shoulders shaking. It had brought back her dreadful ordeal.

Jo took her hands. "Now, what was this smell?"

"Licorice."

"Oh?" Jo thought back. "Yes, you said your captor smelled of it. But, Sally, it's just a sweet." She thought for a moment. Her father had asked the butler about it. He had never said why.

"I wish we knew what happened, Miss Jo. It fair gives me night-mares wondering."

"Lord Reade will find out, Sally."

Sally sighed. "Yes. He is such a clever gentleman."

As Reade approached the stables where he kept Ash, a horseman rode up to him.

"Just the fellow I want to see, Black," Reade said, steadying Ash, who took a dislike to the other horse.

"Spied you riding up Upper Brook Street while I waited for Virden," Winston said. "I hid behind a wall. Didn't want the young lady to see me."

Reade's shoulders tightened. "I want to have words with Virden. Where was he?"

"Visiting the Dalrymple's. He was there for two hours. He's left now. Mitchell is following him."

"Tell me. Did he pick up a fair-haired young woman and drive her to Hyde Park three days ago? And if so, why wasn't I told?"

Black shook his head. "That shift was assigned to the recruit. Richards replaced Goodridge after he hurt his leg."

"And did he report in?"

"Not to my knowledge."

"Get onto Richards right away. I want to know where Virden took the girl and where he left her. Make this a priority, Black. I must see to my horse. Good day to you."

"Good day, milord."

Deeply troubled, Reade entered the stables and dismounted. What was Virden doing at the Dalrymple's for so long? And while Joanna was away? Might he have business with her father? He had discounted Dalrymple as being involved. Was he judging the man by what he knew of his daughter? Dash it all, was he becoming a besotted fool?

As he worked on Ash with the curry brush, he considered Dalrymple. He didn't like Reade, that was obvious. Reade hadn't discovered the reason. Her father seemed an amiable fellow if Reade was any judge. Would he be able to fool his daughter, should he be caught up in something as seedy as this?

While it seemed unlikely, for all her spirited intelligence, Joanna was an innocent. There was much beyond her realm of experience. Did she understand what could have happened to these young women? That Charlotte, even if found, would no longer be the same girl. While he hoped to find the lass quickly and restore her to her family, she had disappeared days ago, which did not bode well for the condition he would find her in, if he found her.

And if this ended badly? Would Joanna forgive him? She seemed to put so much faith in him. That he would care so much, he would never have believed a few short months ago. He allowed himself a pleasurable thought that they might come to mean more to each other. Joanna in his bed. Smiling at him every morning. *Fool!* He did not deserve such a woman. With a pat on Ash's glossy neck, he left the stall. He'd been fooling himself. He would never sink so low as to involve her in his life. That would be the worst thing he ever did.

CHAPTER THIRTEEN

J O WAITED IN the parlor for her father to come home. He smiled as he
entered and drew off his gloves. He seemed very much a man about
Town these days. "Did you enjoy your ride in the park, Jo? Mrs. Millet
and I spent the afternoon at the museum. There's a splendid display of
silver inkpots." He took a chair beside her and described some of the
exhibits.

She didn't mention meeting Reade because he would only disapprove. To keep a secret from him made her uncomfortable. "It sounds
wonderful, Papa. There's something I need to ask you."

"Oh? What is it?"

"Remember when Sally said the man who abducted her smelled of
licorice? You went to ask the butler about it."

He nodded. "Spears confirmed my view of absinthe. Some men
prefer it to whisky or brandy. It's expensive. Sally thought the man
was a gentleman, did she not?"

"She said so. Lord Reade should be told."

He frowned. "Absinth is not uncommon. And what might the
baron have to do with this?"

"I think he works for the government, Papa."

Her father raised his eyebrows. "What area of government?"

"An investigative agent."

"An agent for the Crown? Has he admitted as much?"

"No. I don't expect he would admit it. I've asked for his help to find Charlotte because Mrs. Lincoln refuses to contact Bow Street. She fears a scandal."

"Forget the baron. Agents are a disreputable lot. They kill people. And I've heard unsavory things about Reade."

Reade was a good man. If he weren't, she would know it in her heart. "Lord Reade would not have done what Mrs. Millet accused him of, Papa."

"Mary told you, did she? I can't imagine what reason Mrs. Millet would have to lie to me, can you?"

Jo shook her head miserably.

"You are susceptible. These men hold a certain fascination for many women. I've seen how they watch him at balls. I insist you avoid him."

"But, Papa…"

He stood. "If he finds your friend, Miss Graham, well and good, but he does not need your help."

He walked out the door.

Jo stared despondently after him. This was most unlike her father. He was usually good-tempered. But once he made up his mind about something, he seldom changed it. He would never accept Reade as a son-in-law. Not that a proposal was forthcoming.

A half-hour passed while she sat deep in thought, plucking at the fringe on a cushion. It worried Reade when she told him about Charlotte. He considered her friend's disappearance a serious matter worthy of investigation. But there was no reason she couldn't do something herself. Neither Reade nor her father need know about it. While she wouldn't discover her whereabouts, she might unearth some clue, and she must at least try. Jo rose and went in search of Sally.

"I plan to do some shopping tomorrow, Sally. I'll ask my aunt to join us."

Sally looked up from folding some of Jo's clothes. "Very good, Miss Jo."

"I thought we might go first to Soho Square."

Sally turned to stare at her. "Soho Square, Miss Jo?"

"Yes. You mentioned passing it in the hackney on your way home after that terrifying ordeal. Returning there might jog your memory."

"I've been going over it again and again, and nothing comes, but I'll try."

"Good girl. Think carefully, is there anything, apart from the smell of licorice, that might point to the gentleman you saw in the hall earlier, Mr. Ollerton, as the man who abducted you?" While Jo didn't suspect him, she felt she should at least inquire.

"Oh!" The scarf dropped from Sally's fingers. She put her hands to her cheeks. "Perhaps if I heard his voice again…"

"It was merely conjecture, Sally. I am being unfair to the gentleman. Before we do our shopping, we'll have the jarvey drive around the streets. Perhaps we'll discover where the woman helped you and can continue our search from there."

Sally bent her head over a spencer. "Very well, Miss Jo."

"There is no need to be frightened, Sally, I shan't let anything happen to you, I promise."

Sally shrugged. "They didn't want me. But they might want you, Miss Jo." She glanced up, her expression grave. "I've been talking to the maids belowstairs. They've heard horrible stories."

"I imagine so. And some might be true. But we must not allow our imaginations to run away with us and do our utmost to find Charlotte."

"Yes, Miss Jo."

BLACK CAME TO see Reade again the next morning as he drank coffee in his dining room. "The sun is barely over the yardarm, Black." Reade folded his paper. "What do you have for me?"

"I spoke to Richards, sir. He tells me he followed Virden in the carriage to Hyde Park with the young lady. But Virden outwitted Richards on the way home."

"Bloody hell! He lost him? How the devil did he do that?"

"Richards admits he expected Virden to take the same route home. He feared he'd been spotted, so he rode ahead of him. Virden turned off somewhere. Disappeared into thin air, so to speak."

"Why wasn't I told about this?"

"He didn't report it. Said he thought it unimportant because he found Virden again two hours later at his home."

Reade stared thunderously at Black. "Who recruited this fool?"

"I did, sir," Black said despondently. "As he'd been a Runner, I thought he'd be good."

"Why did he leave Bow Street?"

"There was some trouble. I only discovered it this morning after I spoke to him."

"Never mind that now. Where did Virden disappear? Does Richards know that, at least?"

"A few blocks from Soho Square. Somewhere near a graveyard."

"Richards isn't cut out for this work. Find a replacement. Vet the next one more carefully, Black. There are enough good men looking for work after the war to choose from."

"Yes, sir."

Reade picked up his cup as the door closed. *Soho Square*. Hadn't Joanna's maid, Sally, mentioned passing near it on her way home? He'd have to pay a visit to the brothels. Soho was full of them. Not how he wished to spend the day, but there it was.

CHAPTER FOURTEEN

T HE HACKNEY APPROACHED Solo Square. "We didn't go to the square," Sally said to Jo, her face pressed against the window. "We passed the sign." She tapped the window. "Turn there."

Another few turns, then the air became thick with rancid smells. People crowded into the Berwick Street markets, moving between the livestock pens, the piles of cabbages and potatoes, and stalls selling an odd assortment of wares. "Yes. I remember this market. Keep on this road."

They continued down. "Where to next, Sally?" Jo asked, considering it wise to leave the maid to feel her way.

Sally moaned. "I don't know…"

Aunt Mary held a handkerchief to her nose. "Sally may never remember, Jo."

"Go left!" Sally yelled to the jarvey. "That peddler on the corner with the dog, he was there before. I remember him."

A hunched-over old peddler in a tattered coat sat with his dog on a low wall, his array of goods arranged before him.

The road they followed ended in a smelly ditch.

"I must have made a mistake," Sally said dispiritedly. "The houses were better than these. And there was a big oak tree."

"Well, it was worth a try," Jo said, disappointed. For one exciting moment, she believed they were close.

With a muttered complaint, the jarvey turned the horses. They passed the old man again and continued on toward Oxford Street.

Jo had decided to give up and return to the shops when, at the next cross street, a curricle approached them, drawn by a pair of thoroughbred gray horses.

Reade, in his dark greatcoat and beaver, drew up beside them. A boot on the footboard, he reined in his horses close to them. His expression was thunderous.

"Oh my," Aunt Mary said faintly. "Your father won't be happy about this, Jo."

Reade's stern gaze sought Jo's. He raised his hat and offered a brief greeting. "Have you lost your way? May I assist you?"

"We are going to Golden Square," Jo said weakly, deciding she may as well be hung for a sheep as a lamb, for she had broken her promise to him. "We want to see the statue in the park there. Some believe it is King George II, while others say it's of King Charles II." She was glad she'd listened to her father discussing this very thing with Mary some days ago.

Unconvinced, Reade eyed Jo skeptically. "Parts of Soho are not safe. You are quite a distance from Golden Square. I assume your jarvey knows the way?"

Fortunately, the jarvey, who was apparently losing patience, took umbrage at Reade's suggestion that he was lacking. "I do, as it happens," he said in a heavily ironic tone and slapped the reins.

"Entirely unnecessary, but thank you for your concern," Jo called as their hackney moved away from him.

Reade did not try to follow them. Jo breathed a sigh of relief but expected to hear more of this when she saw him again. She frowned. Must she be made to feel guilty and have to explain herself? He was overbearing. It was a good thing he didn't want to marry her. She sighed and looked back, but he had ridden on.

"Fancy meeting Lord Reade here," Aunt Mary said. "If he says it's not safe, I am sure he must be right. We should return to the shops in Piccadilly."

"And we will, shortly. Forget Golden Square, please, jarvey. Turn around if you please," she instructed.

She could not make out his reply, but she suspected it was disrespectful.

How odd to meet Reade. Did he think Charlotte might be here somewhere? Or was he seeing to some other matter?

"We shall go back to the old peddler with his dog," Jo shouted. "And this time, jarvey, turn left."

The road they took was busy with wagons and drays traveling up and down. "I remember this," Sally said. "If it's the road we came down, we traveled a long way."

They continued for about twenty minutes, crossing Oxford Street. Just as Jo decided they were on a wild goose chase, Sally swiveled on the seat. "That graveyard we just passed. I remember it." She pointed to a narrow road veering off to the right. "Go down that lane!"

Jo gave instructions, and the jarvey obeyed without comment. The lane led them to a cluster of houses set in gardens.

"There's the tree," Sally yelled.

A gigantic oak grew at the side of the road. "Are you sure, Sally?" Jo asked. "One tree might look like another."

"I am. The lady who helped me came out of that house over there. Should I thank her, do you think?"

"One can't just call, it would be bad manners," Aunt Mary said, peering at the two-story house which sat at the end of a short drive with stables behind it. "Only fancy, Jo. That house has yellow-painted shutters and white flowering camellias in pots beside the front door, just like Mrs. Millet's."

Jo stared at the dwelling. Surely, it was too much of a coincidence. Was this Mrs. Millet's house?

"Did you see Mrs. Millet when she came to our house, Sally?"

"No, Miss Jo."

"What was the lady like who helped you?"

"I was so distressed I remember little about her. She wasn't young and had fairish hair."

"Did you give her our address?"

"She asked for it. She wanted to pay the jarvey."

"We'd best go home." It suddenly occurred to Jo that someone inside the house might see them.

Jo looked back as the hackney pulled away from the curb. Surely it couldn't be. If Mrs. Millet had assisted Sally, she would have mentioned the episode to her father. Jo must ask him. And she needed to speak to Reade.

IT WAS THE fifth brothel Reade had visited and the last for the day. He was weary and short-tempered when the madame, a drunkard with dyed red hair, tried to entice him to go with one of her girls. "I am looking for a tall, fair-haired young woman on the slim side."

"Skinny girls ain't always so popular love," she said, eyeing him doubtfully. "Not much up top. We have some curvaceous beauties."

"No."

Her eyes took on a wary look. "Can't help you then, sir. Best you take your business elsewhere."

A bruiser bestirred himself from a chair and stalked over, adopting a menacing attitude.

Reade pulled back his coat to reveal his pistol. "If the girl is here, I will find her and throw you both into Newgate," he said. "Your choice. If you give her up and keep your mouth shut, I'll go easy with you."

"No need for that." She lurched over and clutched his lapel, eyeing him owlishly, breathing gin in his face. "Who says I got 'er?"

"A hunch." He stepped back and pulled his pistol from his breeches, cocking it. "A thorough search will prove it either way."

The bouncer's eyes widened, and he shuffled away, while the madame staggered over and sank down on her chair, folded her arms, and glared at him. "Upstairs, end of the hall on the right. If she's the one you want, I expect payment."

"You'll be lucky not to be in jail by nightfall."

Reade took the rickety stairs two at a time. At the end of the hall, he found the door locked. He put his shoulder to it and heaved, bursting inside the dim room. They'd pasted brown paper over the window. The room smelled of slops and rancid food. As his eyes became accustomed to the gloom, he made out the still form huddled on a grubby mattress on the floor. He ran over and kneeled beside her and eased the long blonde tresses away from her face, which was pale and dirty.

"Don't hurt me," she whispered.

"I'm here to help you," he said gently. "Are you Charlotte Graham?"

She raised herself on her elbows. "I am. Who are you, sir?"

"A friend."

How did you find me?"

"A guess. Now let's get you out of here. Have they been feeding you?"

"Forcing me to eat," she said shakily, leaning heavily on him. "They planned to send me somewhere."

"We'll talk later. Can you walk?"

An arm around her waist, Reade helped her out into the corridor. She stumbled on the stairs. Reade picked her up and carried her down. A shambolic group of women waited in the hall below.

A woman in a grubby dressing gown leered at him. "Miserable thing she is. I can give you a better time, love."

Reade turned to the madame. "I know who brought this young

lady here. If he learns she's gone, I'll come and deal with you. You may not make it as far as jail."

He shouldered his way outside and filled his lungs with fresher air.

"Who are you, kind sir?" Charlotte asked. "How did you…"

"My name is Reade." He tucked her into the curricle and covered her knees with a rug. "But you must thank your friend, Joanna Dalrymple."

"Jo," she gasped out. Her shoulders shuddered, and she covered her face with both hands. "How good she is."

"Yes, indeed." He took up the reins. *Jo.* It suited her. He was feeling a good deal better as he drove the curricle out of the ramshackle streets. If he'd blown the investigation and they lost the leader of the gang, so be it. This young woman was going home. He glanced at her sitting quietly beside him. "Are you all right?"

She dropped her hands and gave him a lopsided smile. "I am. I can't thank you enough."

"No need."

"Mr. Virden left me there."

"I know."

"Will you arrest him?"

"In due course. He doesn't act alone. You might help us."

"I'll do anything. Just tell me what you want."

"We'll talk about it later. I'm taking you home, but I don't want anyone but Mrs. Lincoln to know you're there. We'll keep it a secret for now."

She shivered and cast him an anxious glance. "Do you think they'll come to find me?"

"I'll place a guard to watch the house."

He handed her his handkerchief. Charlotte dabbed her eyes and fell back against the seat, exhausted, silent tears running down her face.

Reade clamped down his jaw and prayed for the opportunity to take his fists to Crispin Virden.

CHAPTER FIFTEEN

AFTER LUNCHEON, AUNT Mary retired to her bedchamber, complaining too much excitement gave her a headache. Jo guiltily sent for Feverfew and left her aunt to sleep.

As Jo paced the parlor, a note arrived from Reade. She left the house and flew down the steps to catch the man who'd delivered the missive into the butler's hands.

"Wait!" she called as he walked away up the street. "I want you to take a message back to Lord Reade," she instructed him. "Please wait in the hall for a moment."

"Yes, miss."

Spears stood poker-faced at the door, but Jo still felt his displeasure as she ushered the man inside. She hurried into the empty library. This was her father's favorite room, his pipes arranged on the leather-topped desk, but he had gone out again with Mrs. Millet. Jo had been waiting impatiently for him to return.

She scanned Reade's note.

"Oh!" Her breath caught in her throat, and she fell onto the leather chair beside the desk. He had found Charlotte. She read it twice, fearing she'd misunderstood his words. But it was true. A tear splattered onto the page. Jo dipped the quill in the inkwell. She scratched him a hasty note, telling him she would be near the Brook Street gate at Hyde Park at three o'clock in the hope he could meet her.

Jo left the library and handed the note to the ginger-haired gentle-man who'd introduced himself as Mr. Black. "Please ensure Lord Reade gets this as soon as possible."

"I will, Miss Dalrymple, but it might be a while, he has an appointment with the Prince Regent."

"Tell him I will wait as long as I can." It concerned her what her father would say when he heard. When Black left, she returned to the library and read Reade's note again.

They had restored Charlotte to her home in good health. There were no details. Jo would have to wait to satisfy her curiosity. She roamed the room, removing scarlet and gold bound books from the shelves and then returning them with nary a glance. Was Mrs. Millet involved in Sally's abduction? Was it she who persuaded the abductor to let her maid go? It seemed preposterous, and yet she could not discount it. She had never liked the woman. Jo didn't have a good reason, except she'd sensed Mrs. Millet was insincere. But her father was unlikely to believe anything she told him on such sketchy evidence.

The door knocker echoed through the hall.

Jo darted out just as the butler closed the door again. "Another note, Miss Dalrymple," Spears said as if such a thing was insupportable.

"Thank you, Spears," Jo unfolded it and read it. "My father will not be dining at home," she explained. Her father and Mrs. Millet would dine after viewing an exhibition of Turner's artworks. He had spent almost the entire day with the woman, and now the evening. Was she becoming dear to him? He'd be distressed if they discovered she was not who she appeared.

Spears nodded somberly. "I shall instruct Cook."

"Thank you." At least she didn't have to tell her father she was walking to the park. He would forbid her. "Please send Sally to my bedchamber."

Spears murmured an assent. Never deviating from his usual upright stance, he shifted his foot as if it pained him, drawing her attention. Jo admitted she had never really looked at the butler. His hair was turning white, his face deeply lined. He was a good deal older than she first thought.

"My father could be late tonight. Have a footman answer the door, Mr. Spears. I don't expect anyone else to call today."

She thought the suggestion that he needed rest might ruffle his feathers, but his usually indifferent gaze focused on hers with warm surprise. "I believe I will. Thank you, Miss Dalrymple."

How wrong one could be about people, she thought as she climbed the stairs. But she was not wrong about Mrs. Millet. She was sure of it.

Jo had taken her lilac walking dress out of the wardrobe when Sally came in. "Only imagine, Sally, Charlotte has been found safe and well! I went to tell Aunt Mary, but she is still asleep."

Sally clapped her hands to her cheeks. "That's such wonderful news, Miss Jo."

"I need to see Lord Reade. I've sent him a letter. We must return to the park."

Sally took the dress from her and shook it out. "We aren't to ride this time, Miss Jo?"

"No. I'll leave a message for Aunt Mary." She glanced at her watch. "It's three-fifteen. The park doesn't become busy until five. Hopefully, we won't have to wait long," she said almost to herself as she shrugged out of her morning dress.

In the park, dark threatening clouds banked up in the sky, the wind stirring the branches. How foolish not to bring an umbrella. She had been so distracted; she hadn't noticed the change in the weather. The chance of rain had kept the *ton* away, for the park was almost deserted.

They waited an hour as the sky darkened. Reade did not come.

Had he received her note? Mr. Black would ensure he got it. And Reade would never let her down. She rubbed her arms. "I imagine the Regent has delayed him."

They waited a further fifteen minutes. "I've just had a thought, Sally," Jo said. "Lord Reade might have driven through the Hyde Park gate in his curricle."

"Shall I walk over there?" Sally asked.

"No. You wait here. I'll go." Jo hurried toward Rotten Row. She searched the South Carriage Drive for a dark blue curricle driven by a pair of gray horses, and he wasn't on horseback. The traffic thinned as rain clouds hovered overhead. The rest of the people deserted the park. Thinking Reade might have arrived and was with Sally, she turned to go back. Someone hailed her.

Jo spun around, expecting to see Reade.

A carriage stopped, and the door opened. Beckoned forward, Jo hurried over, but it was Mr. Ollerton seated inside. "I thought I saw you, Miss Dalrymple. Only fancy. What are you doing in the park on your own?"

"Good day to you, Mr. Ollerton. I am here with my maid. She is over by the Brook Street gate. I am looking for a...a friend."

A drop of rain splattered on her bonnet.

"The weather has turned nasty. I have an umbrella here. Please allow me to give it to you."

Jo approached him. "How kind, thank you." She walked over to the door and held out her hand.

Ollerton's gloved hand snaked out and grabbed her wrist. He pulled Jo inside the carriage. She opened her mouth to scream but was roughly shoved to the floor.

Gripped by sheer terror, for a moment she couldn't think, couldn't speak, and then she gasped, "Your name's not Ollerton. You're Virden, aren't you?"

"Be quiet. I have a knife, and I won't hesitate to use it."

Icy dread flooded her veins as the carriage juddered forward. Jo's stomach churned. Sally hadn't seen her with Ollerton. Reade wouldn't know what had happened to her. "Let me go. I'm no good to you."

"You underestimate yourself."

She swallowed on a sob. "What do you want?"

"You will know soon enough. Finding you alone is most fortuitous."

"My maid will have seen you. She will run home and alert my father."

She felt cold steel on the back of her neck and shuddered. "Do not toy with me," he snarled. "Were you responsible for snatching your friend Charlotte Graham away from the brothel?"

The carriage was now traveling fast, rocking from side to side. "No, but I'm glad she is safe. You are a monster!"

"I saw you in the street outside my house. How did you know I lived there?"

Jo gasped and raised her head to stare at him. "Your house?"

He pushed her down. "Enough! You shall tell me all about it when we arrive."

"Let me go. You can't get away with this."

"Ordinarily, I wouldn't consider you, it's true. You're a bad risk. But my plans have changed."

"What do you want from me?" Jo asked again. But she feared his answer.

"If you don't be quiet, you'll come to regret it."

Jo shivered and buried her head in her arms as a hot tear seeped onto her cheek. Where was he taking her?

READE SPENT SEVERAL hours with the Prince Regent, placating him after a long diatribe ended with a demand to be told about the investigation. He assured the prince it was advancing steadily. He wasn't required to go into details, but Prinny's interest puzzled him. Usually, criminal activity that involved the lower-classes or the poor didn't capture his attention unless it was a threat to royalty or the government.

Reade arrived home in the late afternoon to change for the evening. He found Black waiting for him. He handed Reade a note. "From Miss Dalrymple, sir."

A brief missive that gave him no clue as to the reason she wished to see him. He snatched up his hat and rushed out to hail a hackney.

When he and Black reached the Brook Street gate, a woebegone figure stood in the rain. He asked the jarvey to wait and ran over to Sally. "Where is your mistress?"

Sally's pelisse was wet, and her bonnet hung limply around her face. She trembled and struggled to speak.

Reade glanced around with a sense of foreboding. No sign of Joanna. He pulled off his greatcoat and hung it over the girl's shoulders.

"Miss Jo went off to look for your carriage over an hour ago, my lord. When she didn't come back, I searched for her. But she's gone."

He felt the hair lift off the back of his neck. "Gone? Are you sure?" He spun around. The rain had cleared the park of all but a few determined horse riders. "Why did she want to see me, Sally? Do you know?"

"We had the hackney go back the way I came home on that awful day," Sally said, tripping over her words. "We found the house where the lady helped me. Miss Hatton said she thought it might be Mrs. Millet's house because of the camellias and the shutters. Miss Jo thought you should know about it."

Reade raised his eyebrows. "Who is Mrs. Millet?"

"Mr. Dalrymple hired Mrs. Millet to help Jo with her debut."

Things slid into place. This Mrs. Millet was Mrs. Virden. Reade eased his tight shoulders. Had Virden learned of Charlotte's rescue? Was Jo in danger? But he was letting his emotions rule his head. They tailed Virden. His man would contact him, and it better be soon.

As Reade's hackney took Sally to Upper Brook Street, Black appeared in a curricle. He brought his horse close to intercept them.

Reade jumped down. "Who is following Virden?"

"Goodridge. Said his leg was better."

"And?" Reade waited, fearing the worst.

"Virden outmaneuvered him. It appears he has conceived a means of escape."

"Good lord!" Reade yelled. "Can I count on no one? Where did this happen?"

"Goodridge followed him to the park in his coach," Black said. "Didn't stay above a few minutes while Goodridge waited outside the park gates."

"Was he alone? Did he meet anyone?"

"Goodridge didn't see anyone with him."

"Go on." Reade motioned to him.

"Then he drove through Soho. Apparently, there's a way through a cemetery. Goodridge turned a corner, and he had vanished. Virden either knows he's followed or is taking no chances."

"The graveyard could be the one near Mrs. Millet's house," Sally said.

"I think you might be right, Sally. Well done. But I must leave you here. Can I rely on you to tell Mr. Dalrymple? Do it gently, please. I will return Jo to them as soon as I can."

"Mr. Dalrymple dines with Mrs. Millet this evening. But Miss Hatton is at home."

"Then inform Miss Hatton, Sally, and say I shall have Jo home directly."

Sally went up the steps, and Reade leaped into the curricle with Black.

"That devil has taken her," he growled. "Take me to the stables. I'll ride to Virden's house, although I don't expect to find him there."

"Move on!" Black slapped the reins.

As Black drove, Reade tried to think where Virden might hide Jo. It wouldn't be the brothel where he'd kept Charlotte. Did they use other such places? He dragged in a breath at the dispiriting thought. Their meeting was to take place tomorrow. Somewhere near the docks. He must find Virden. Reade did not intend for Jo to endure a night with him or in a brothel. He would find her if he had to employ the large number of ex-army men he knew to help him.

"Pull Rivenstock in for questioning at Bow Street," he said through his teeth as Black pulled up outside the stables. "He might be a lord, but I'm not above getting rough if threats don't work."

CHAPTER SIXTEEN

"UP," VIRDEN ORDERED.

Jo raised herself to gaze out the window as the coach juddered down a drive. It pulled up outside the house Jo had discovered that morning. Mrs. Millet's house! Was it only this morning? It seemed such a long time ago.

"Right! Out! We can't stay long." Virden dug his fingers into her arm and pulled her out the door onto the ground. Jo almost fell. She fought to stay on her feet as he hauled her along.

"Who is Mrs. Millet to you?" she asked when they reached the porch.

"She's Mrs. Virden, and she's my mother."

"*Mrs. Virden.*" Her breath hitched, and she tried to pull away from him. "What do you want with me?"

"You are the holy grail, my dear. I was on the lookout for someone as things have become desperate. And there you were." With a hand on her arm, he opened the door and hustled her into the hall. "Good thing we let all the servants go after you and that maid of yours popped up uninvited. Upstairs."

In a bedchamber, he forced Jo onto a chair. She sat watching while he removed clothes from drawers and packed a portmanteau. Her terror had subsided a little, and her curiosity took over. She wanted the truth. All of it. "Why did you kidnap Charlotte?" She still didn't know how Reade found her friend.

"You know about her then." He tucked his brushes into the case. "When I returned your maid, I needed to replace her to appease our buyers. We were sending your friend Charlotte to Algiers."

Jo shuddered. "Why would you do such a thing?"

"The slave market. A wealthy sheik wants to expand his harem. Fair-haired women are in demand there. I haven't found another suitable girl since last year."

Her blood ran cold. She shivered and searched for a means of escape.

He noticed the movement and turned to her, his eyes cold. "Don't think you can fool me. Stay where you are, or I will tie you up."

"Was that girl you took Anabel Riley?"

"It was some chit my mother enticed from the street."

Jo hated him more deeply than she believed possible. He cared for no one but himself.

"So, your name isn't Ollerton."

"Ollerton was a gentleman I knew who died. Virden was my stepfather's name. Millet is my mother's maiden name." His face pinched, and Jo saw Mrs. Millet in his features. She held her head in her hands. *Oh, Papa!*

"Our plan was for Mother to marry your father and then assist him into the grave, or I abduct you and hold you for ransom. But none of that will happen now. It's got far too hot in London for me. I need money, a ticket out of here."

"You are vile."

"You do not understand how ruthless these people can be," he said in a pitiful tone. "They will have me killed and throw my body into the Thames should I fail again." He looked triumphant. "But I now have you."

"Me?" Jo's lungs squeezed as she struggled for breath.

Virden glared at her, a look of madness in his eyes while fingering the long thin stiletto in his hands. "A pretty redhead should delight a sheik. It won't be so bad if you please your master, that is. Look on the bright side, you will have his other wives for company." He frowned. "And if he insists on a blonde, I shall sell you in the slave market."

Jo leaned back on the chair, her heart beating hard. "How did someone like you gain entry to *ton* balls? You belong in the rookery of St. Giles."

His features contorted, making him ugly.

"You are lucky I must hand you over in perfect condition," he said, his voice a low growl. "My mother and I have friends among the *ton*. They enjoy our charming company at their pathetic balls but wouldn't shed a tear if we ended up in the poor house. And woe-betide me if I asked to marry one of their daughters."

"So, another lie when you said Viscount Cranswick was your father. There is no Julian."

Virden scowled heavily. "The viscount is my father," he spat out. "And Julian is his son. But he never cared about me, his bastard second son. My mother was his mistress, and he treated both us like dirt. I planned to kill him before I left England, but there'll be no time for that now. Agents of the crown are on to us, it seems."

"And they're very close behind you."

"They'll be too late. We sail to Plymouth on the morning tide, and on to Algiers."

Jo swallowed, her throat horribly dry. "You are leaving your mother behind to face them. They might kill her."

A shadow passed over his features. "The east doesn't appeal to her. She prefers to remain in England. She's clever, my mother, she will find a means to escape the law. Mother has excellent family connections, you know." He snapped the lock on the bag shut. "Enough talk. We'll have plenty of time for that on the boat. Should you feel like talking."

"I won't be on that boat." Jo fought not to let his words make her desperate. Would Reade know where to look for her? And if he did, would he come too late?

Virden stood and observed her. "You're a spirited one. You will please them, although it's a pity about your maid. I wanted her for myself, but Mother wisely insisted on sending her back."

"Your mother would never stand a chance with my father," Jo said. "He is merely amusing himself with her."

"I'd shut my mouth if I were you."

Tears pricked Jo's eyes, and she lowered her head in case he saw them. She would never give him that satisfaction.

Virden pushed her into another bedchamber, which was obviously his mother's. He pulled a sack from under the bed. "Gold." He weighed it in his hands, then pulled the drawstring open to peer inside. "I will need this."

While the bag of gold distracted him, Jo pulled her locket over her head. Her fingers closed on it as she held it in her palm. "You are stealing your mother's money."

He shrugged. "I'd leave her a bit, but she won't be back here. She will get by. Has a talent for it, as I told you. Still a good-looking woman, my mother. Can mix with anyone."

"She'll get on well with those in Newgate then," Jo said.

"Don't provoke me. I warn you." He tucked the gold inside the portmanteau and stood. "It's time to go. We don't want to miss the boat, do we?"

The coach they'd come in waited in the drive. Dressed in an oil-skin, a bulky figure hunched over on the box as the rain pelted down. Jo let the locket slip from her fingers onto the porch. Reade had once commented on it. Perhaps he would remember it and know she'd been here. She clung to the hope he'd find her. For if she lost all hope, the fight would drain out of her. And she intended to fight Virden the first chance she got.

In the carriage, Virden made Jo lie on the squab beneath a rug. It smelled chokingly of dust and horse. Trying not to cough, she thought over what he had told her. Who was behind this gang of procurers? It was not Virden, he wasn't smart or powerful. Nor would it be his mother. A woman wouldn't have overseas connections. If Reade had been investigating them, he might have some knowledge of where Virden was taking her. But dusk was not far off, and at dawn the following morning, the tide would turn and sweep her away from England. It seemed impossible to believe. Too scared to cry, she put her fist to her mouth as her throat tightened on unshed tears.

WHEN BLACK WENT to arrest Rivenstock, Reade saddled Ash. Within minutes, he was on the road to the Virdens' house.

The cottage had a shuttered look. No servant answered the door. Reade broke a window and climbed inside, moving from room to room, gun cocked. In the upstairs bedchamber there was evidence of a hasty departure, but no sign of Jo. When he emerged again through the front door, something bright caught his eye, lying on the porch. He bent and picked it up. A gold heart-shaped locket. He released a slow breath. The last time he'd seen this dainty piece of jewelry was around Jo's slender neck.

He threaded the fragile chain through his fingers. At first, he feared Virden had ripped it from her, but he was wrong. The clasp was fastened. Might she have dropped it on purpose? As a sign? It told him Verdin had brought her here, but not where he took her. With a curse, he tucked it into his waistcoat pocket.

No staff and no horses in the stables. Virden was on the run, and Jo was with him. Why? Did he intend to sell her as he had so many before? In that case, he didn't intend to return here. They were shipping Charlotte overseas, was that Virden's intention for Jo? Reade groaned. His men would have to watch the docks. He'd need a shipping list. Boats departing London within the next week.

Mounting Ash again, he rode to Bow Street. He had lost too many he cared about. Well, it would not end that way. Not this time. He would find Jo and restore her safely to her home. If he didn't, his life wouldn't be worth living.

In the mood to draw blood, even should it be aristocratic, Reade set Ash at a gallop and rode through the streets toward Covent Garden.

CHAPTER SEVENTEEN

THE RAIN EASED to a drizzle as Virden's coach traveled along beside the brick walls rimming the docks where tradesmen and port workers unloaded sugar, tobacco, and spices from trading vessels in the soot-filled air. Through the darkening sky, a sea of masts could be seen rocking on the Thames in the Pool of London. The recent deluge formed impenetrable black puddles over the ground.

Verdin's coachman stopped at the mouth of a lane too narrow for the vehicle to proceed farther. Alighting on the pavement, Virden paid him, then took hold of Jo's arm and hurried her along. Her knees were weak, and she feared they'd give way while her nerves jumped at the noise from a tavern on the corner where drunken sailors and steve-dores argued or sang shanties off-key. If she escaped Virden, could she find safety among them? She was willing to try.

Virden unlocked a door set in a grimy brick wall and pushed Jo inside. The lack of a window made the space dark and gloomy. It smelled of unwashed bodies and rats. The only furniture, a rickety table and four mismatched chairs and a filthy mattress on the floor against one wall. The stub of candle he lit threw flickering halos over the discolored walls, drawing them in, making the room seem even smaller. Virden hadn't locked the door. But if she tried to flee now, he would only hurt her. She must bide her time.

He gestured for her to sit and slumped into a chair. Jo as far away from him as possible, but she remained within reach. His earlier bluster had ebbed away during the journey. The prospect of leaving these shores must have lost its appeal.

She rested her elbows on the table and studied him from beneath her lashes. How might she outwit him? When she shuffled her feet to test him, his head came up sharply.

"Don't even think of trying to escape. You are my ticket out of here. I don't intend to lose you."

Did he expect someone? "Are we to sit here all night?" she asked. "I'm hungry, and this chair is hard."

"Stop your whining. There's the bed if you prefer it."

"No, thank you. Lice and rats don't appeal, but they're no worse than you."

He scowled and opened his mouth to rebuke her, but a clatter out in the street brought him to his feet. He hurried over to the door, opened it a crack, and peered out.

It occurred to her that rather than expecting someone, he feared it. He had abandoned not just his mother, but his gang of crooks. If they discovered what he was up to, surely they'd come after him? She shivered. She hoped they wouldn't. For that would seal her fate.

Virden shut the door and returned to his chair, relief etched on his face as he sat down.

"Are you afraid someone has discovered what you're up to and come after you?" she asked, watching him, chin resting in her palm.

He glared at her. "Not before the meeting tomorrow at noon. We'll be long gone by then."

As he seemed prepared to talk, Jo pursued another topic. "How many of you are there?"

"Nosey, aren't you? Four, counting my mother and me, plus a few henchmen from the rookeries eager to do our bidding. We have a good number of girls in London brothels now. But the big money is not to be made here in England."

"Who are those two men?"

He raised his brows. "Now, wouldn't you like to know?"

She shrugged. "I suppose you're afraid I'll tell someone."

"Who will you tell? The captain of the ship?" he sneered. "Lord Rivenstock is one of them."

The horrible fat man who held the first ball Jo attended. She could believe it of him. "I understood gentlemen had a code of honor."

"How naïve you country girls are. Our leader is related to the king."

She slowly shook her head. "Really?"

He narrowed his eyes. "You doubt it? It is Roland, Viscount Lothian. Guineamen made him rich," Verdin said moodily. "But there's too much opposition to the trade, so he is keen to diversify where he doesn't have to get his hands dirty."

"What are Guineamen?"

"The slave ships from the Guinea coast."

Jo failed to hide her shock and disgust.

Verdin looked pleased. "I've impressed you. As you can see, I'm in excellent company."

"But you're leaving. And you can never return to England. Or see your mother again," she said reflectively. "Although I imagine she won't want to see you, will she?"

He leaned over and gave her a stinging slap across the cheek.

Jo fell back, her hand to her face. "*Brute.*"

"That will teach you to button your lip, girl. I warn you not to insult me again. We have weeks before we arrive in Tangiers. So, keep control of yourself."

Jo rested her head in her arms. Riling him achieved nothing. Best to wait and see what chances the night might bring.

DUSK HAD FALLEN, and Reade's impatience and temper got the better of him as he stood in the Bow Street room, with Black, watching Rivenstock quiver. The lord's demands for his solicitor had fallen on deaf ears. It was Reade's hope when Rivenstock discovered himself one step from a Newgate holding cell, where his title was unlikely to protect him for long, it might loosen his tongue.

Reade rested his knuckles on the table before him. "You won't enjoy being packed into a cell with cutthroats. They live by a certain code which might not tally with yours."

"They'll appreciate that diamond ring, gold fob, and watch," Black said. "And your pretty waistcoat buttons. Pearl, are they?"

"Why am I here?" Rivenstock rubbed a hand across his eyes. "What do you want from me?"

"Give up the names of your gang, and things will go better for you," Reade said. "Where would Virden take a young woman?"

"He's taken a girl? How should I know where he'd go with her?" Rivenstock's attempt at surprise evaporated when Reade grabbed his collar.

His hands tightened, and Rivenstock's face turned crimson. "Where would he take her? A Soho brothel?"

Rivenstock struggled and gasped. "I can't tell you! No matter what you do to me. I don't know!"

"Tomorrow's meeting. Where is it to take place?"

Rivenstock eyed him aloofly. "I'll have you know I am a close friend of the Prince Regent."

Black kicked Rivenstock's chair, sending it back against the wall. The man clutched the sides, his eyes wide. "Lord Reade would have the Regent's ear long before he listens to the likes of you."

The man's shoulders sagged. "If I tell you, will you let me speak to my solicitor before I go before the magistrate? I am a lord of the realm. You cannot send me to Newgate."

"Providing you get that far. There's many a slip between cup and lip." Reade eyed the overweight, indulgent man before him. His fingers itched to take him apart, but he wasn't about to waste time on him, and he needed that information. "Answer Black's questions, and I promise you we will send for your solicitor. Now, the address of the meeting place or our patience is at an end."

"Cannon Lane, near the West India docks. Noon tomorrow."

"Tell me about this meeting, you shivering lump of lard," Black demanded as Reade strode out of the room.

"A matter of business on hand," Rivenstock unwisely replied. His scream of pain echoed down the hallway after Reade.

Was there a chance he'd find Jo in Cannon Lane? There was nowhere else to look except the brothels, and there were dozens of them. He groaned as he ran to get Ash, who he'd stabled nearby. As he mounted the horse, a paralyzing thought struck him. Business on hand, Rivenstock had said. Their business was sending fair English women to the slave markets of eastern countries. That meant they had a woman in mind. Was it to be Jo?

Reade nudged Ash into a gallop.

CHAPTER EIGHTEEN

HOW LONG HAD she been in this windowless room? Jo had lost track of time. Her neck and her back ached from being constantly tense. She raised her head from her arms to see if Virden still watched her. He sat with his hands shoved into his waistcoat pockets, looking contemplative. He appeared calmer. Did he think himself safe? She supposed he did, for in a few scant hours, they would board the ship. Panic shortened her breath. Somehow, she must escape. At least try, even if he hurt her. But after a glance at the implacable man, her confidence sank to rock bottom.

"We shall breakfast onboard," he said in a conversational tone as if they were about to take a pleasant sea voyage. "You can sleep in the cabin as long as you wish."

"I won't eat or sleep." She wouldn't give him the satisfaction, although her stomach felt hollow, and she was dreadfully tired.

He frowned. "You will. I won't have you arriving in a bedraggled state. I shall buy you a gown." He tilted his head and observed her with shrewd eyes. "Green and gold silk. It will become you with your red hair."

"And to think I once considered you a gentleman."

Verdin's eyes burned with fury. She had discovered his weakness. Could she use it to distract him? "I am one," he snarled. "But English society turns its back on a gentleman's bastard."

"They have shown a good deal of commonsense in this case." Jo pushed back out of the reach of his raised arm. As she expected, with a cry of anger, he threw back his chair and stood to advance around the table. "I warned you not to anger me again. Now you'll be sorry."

Fear made Jo move faster. She sent her chair crashing on its side in his path. It tripped him up, and he came down hard with a cry as she ran to the door. Wrenching it open, she bolted out into the street, then gasped as the pelting rain blinded her. Night had fallen. She stumbled toward the lighted tavern, unsure of the reception she'd get but no longer caring. Anywhere was better than where she'd been.

Her wet clothes clinging to her, she ran inside. A dozen sets of male eyes stared at her, the air laden with hops, smoke, wet wool, and sweat.

Jo pushed a lock of hair out of her eyes. She ran over to the tavern-keeper, who was filling tankards with ale. "Please, could you help me?"

He signaled to a woman perched on a man's lap. "You are needed, Becky."

Becky slipped off the man's knee and received a slap on the bottom. She sashayed over to Jo. "You're in a state, aren't you, luv?"

Jo stared at the door, expecting Virden to burst in at any moment. "Yes, I…"

"Not here. Come upstairs. You need to dry off."

Jo followed her up the stairs to a tiny bedchamber. A small casement window overlooked the street. She stared down through the rain. A group of people scurried past, but she couldn't pick out Virden among them.

"Now, what can I do for you, pet?" Becky held out a bit of toweling.

"Thank you." Jo took it and attempted to dry her hair. "A man abducted me from the park. He is out there looking for me."

"But what are you doin' down 'ere, luv?"

"It's a long story. I want to go home, but I don't have any money."

"You can turn a trick with one 'o them downstairs."

Jo stared at her. "What?"

Becky shrugged, looking amused. "Thought so. Gently reared, they call the likes of you. Mayfair, is it?"

"Yes, how did you…?

"Your fine clothes for one." Opening a drawer, she took out a leather drawstring bag. She extracted some coins. "Doubt I'll see this again. No matter. Twill be me good deed of the day, won't it."

"I'll return your money, Becky. I promise."

Becky dropped two silver coins in Jo's hand. "Two bob should do it. I'll come outside with you and whistle up a 'ackney. But few come 'ere this time o' night."

Jo tensed. "The man who kidnapped me will wait out there."

Becky removed a knife from a drawer and hid it in the folds of her knitted shawl. "Then 'e'll be sorry, won't 'e?"

Her heart in her mouth, Jo followed Becky downstairs.

"Hey, Becky, why don't you bring yer friend over," a rough-looking man called. "She looks like she could do with a drink." His mates boisterously agreed.

"No thanks, Bert," Becky said. "She's not for the likes of you."

"Eh?" Bert lumbered to his feet.

"Fred?" Becky turned to the tavern-keeper. A big beefy man, he stepped forward with a lump of wood in his hand and cast a warning glance at Bert.

"Forget it." Bert shook his head and sunk back into his chair.

Jo shivered as she and Becky ventured out into the rain and walked toward the main road, which ran the length of the harbor's edge.

A man appeared from the shelter of a doorway opposite.

"It's him," Jo whispered.

"Don't like the look of 'im." Becky turned away. "Better I get Fred."

"No! Don't leave me, Becky!"

Becky disappeared into the tavern. Jo went to follow, but Virden was quickly upon her. "Thought you'd run away from me, did you? I'll teach you a lesson." He thrust her back toward the room. Jo struggled and struck at his face with her nails. With a curse, he pinned her arms and lifted her off her feet.

A clamor behind them made Virden turn. Becky and three men burst out of the tavern and spilled onto the street.

"She's my wife. Mind your business," Virden cried.

The men stopped. "'e's a toff," one of them said. The men lost interest and filed back into the warmth and dry of the tavern.

"You didn't say he was your hubby, luv," Becky called.

A clatter of hooves and a horse rider galloped out of the dark. *Reade!* Was she dreaming?

Virden pushed her away and ran up the lane.

Jo screamed. "Reade! He's got a knife."

Reade jumped down from his horse and took off at a run after Virden, who'd almost reached the door to his room.

Becky hurried over to her. "Friend 'o yours is 'e?"

Jo nodded.

"I should like to be his friend." Becky grasped her arm. "Come inside out of the rain."

"No, I can't get any wetter. You go in, Becky." She pushed the money back into Becky's hands. "And, thank you!"

Stiff with fear, Jo stood alone in the halo of light cast over the street from the open doorway.

Reade brought Virden down in a flying tackle. The villain scrambled away from him. Back on his feet, he rounded on him.

If only she could help, but Jo could only watch helplessly and pray.

READE NEEDED VIRDEN alive. He aimed his gun at the scoundrel's chest. "It's over, Virden."

"You're not taking me. You'll have to shoot me," Virden snarled.

It would be very satisfying to kill him after what he and his cronies had done to those women and Jo. But neither Virden nor Rivenstock were the mastermind of this cruel enterprise. If Black failed to get the leader's name from Rivenstock, who appeared too terrified to reveal it, they might never find him.

Reade replaced his gun in his pocket and advanced on Virden, raising his fists.

With a savage laugh, Virden came at him, a knife flashing in his hand. It curved upward in a wicked arc, aiming for Reade's heart.

Reade leaped to one side, avoiding the blade, then caught and clamped Virden's wrist in both hands. The knife skittered away out of reach. Bending over, Reade hoisted Virden onto his shoulder, throwing him hard to the ground. Turning, he quickly realized there was no need for haste. Virden lay with his head at an odd angle where he'd hit the edge of the gutter. Reade cursed under his breath.

He bent and went through the man's pockets. Virden's head lolled back, and his sightless eyes stared up at him. Reade found the fake passports, tickets on the Seaward bound for Algiers, and a drawstring purse filled with coins. He rose to his feet.

Jo walked up the lane toward him, her clothing soaked, bareheaded, her hair tumbling over her shoulders. She came to look down on Virden, then hugged herself and shuddered. "Is he dead?"

Reade slipped off his coat and wrapped it around her. "I'm afraid he is."

"I'm not sorry," she said through chattering teeth. "He was taking me away from England. The boat leaves on the morning tide."

Her anguish knocked the breath out of him. "I'm not sorry he's dead, sweetheart, but he had information valuable to us. Did he leave anything in that room?"

"Yes. A portmanteau. There's a bag of gold in it."

"Stand in the shelter of the doorway. I won't be long."

Reade dragged Virden's body inside. Someone would come for him tomorrow. His coat hung over a chair. Reade checked the pockets. Nothing. Picking up the weighty portmanteau, he went out, shutting the door behind him.

"Reade, Virden told me about the others."

He gazed down at her. "Lord Rivenstock?"

"Yes, and Lord Lothian."

"Lothian?" Reade raised his eyebrows. No wonder the regent was interested. Disillusioned, it occurred to Reade that Prinny may have turned a blind eye to Lothian's sordid activities. But he would not want a scandal of this magnitude erupting. Not when he was so unpopular.

He put an arm around Jo's shoulders. "That's of immense help to us, Jo. I need to get you home before you catch a chill."

"Let me speak to Becky first. I want to thank her," she said as they approached the tavern. "She helped me, gave me money for the fare home."

"Good of her. But not tonight." Raucous laughter floated out. A tavern was no haven for a beautiful girl. It didn't bear thinking about.

Ash stood patiently, waiting for him. Reade strapped the small portmanteau onto the back of the saddle, then lifted Jo onto Ash and mounted behind her. His arms around her, he took up the reins and rode the horse back along the road.

Jo was so small and soft in his arms; his heart thudded wildly. How close he'd come to losing her. She leaned her head back against his chest as he urged the horse into a canter along the dark streets. A rush of exhilaration rushed through him; she was safe. He wanted to hug her.

"What does Lord Lothian look like?" she asked.

"Lothian? Tall, thin, with white hair."

"I saw him at Astley's Amphitheater with Mrs. Millet. I suppose she brought him to have a look at us," she said with bitterness in her voice. "She and Virden planned to get their hands on my father's money. Either Virden was to kidnap me and demand a ransom, or she would entice my father into marriage. And then," her voice lowered, "kill him."

His arm tightened around her. He had no words.

When they arrived at the Mayfair townhouse, candlelight shone from all the downstairs windows and the servants' quarters below. The door opened, and Mr. Dalrymple rushed down the steps, followed by Jo's aunt and the butler.

"Jo! Dear heaven, are you all right?"

"Yes, Papa," she said wearily. "Lord Reade saved me."

Her father seized Reade's hand and shook it vigorously. "I'm so grateful, my lord. Come inside, share a meal with us."

"I regret I cannot stay, sir, as I'm needed elsewhere. I will call tomorrow afternoon."

"Please do, my lord. I cannot thank you enough for saving my daughter." He cleared his throat, his eyes watering. "Jo is precious to me."

Jo stood silently by, swaying on her feet. Reade feared she would fall, and he would catch her. And when he did, that would be it. He doubted he'd let her go again. And while the lord knew he wanted her, he needed to think hard about what was best for her. And understand what she might want for herself.

He bedded Ash down in his stall and hailed a hackney to Bow Street. Knowing Black, he expected to find him still there. It was a delicate situation. Once he learned all that Black had got from Rivenstock, he would relay the information to the Home Office in the morning. The news would not be well received, but it was out of his hands.

Prinny would be irate, although Reade suspected he already knew.

He was glad to be finished with the dirty business. It left him with a nasty taste in his mouth. His work for the crown had been rewarding, but recent events made him feel jaded and disenchanted.

Black, reliable as ever, awaited him there. Rivenstock had cracked and confessed to his and the Virdens' culpability but clamped his lips on any mention of Lothian. Perhaps he feared the viscount more than the law.

Some hours later, after a meal and a stiff whisky, Reade wearily climbed into his bed. The fear of losing Jo had almost ripped him apart. He never wanted to suffer that again. Cartwright had accused him of leaving his heart on the battlefield. Brutal, but it held a degree of truth, although he wouldn't take it from anyone but Cartwright.

Reade didn't consider himself a hero. And not after the last decisive battle which won the war. A family friend had written to implore Reade to watch over his impetuous young heir, Miles, who had taken the king's shilling and joined up without his father's consent. Reade had failed. It was two years ago, but the sickening memory of what happened that day never lost its grip on him. And the nightmares persisted, making him wake up in a sweat every morning.

While the candle sent dancing shadows around the room, he lay back and placed an arm over his eyes. He invited it back. Maybe if he dealt with it now, he could sleep.

It might have been yesterday, not 1815. Sunday, June 18th. Two hundred thousand soldiers met on a few acres of land near the small Belgian town of Waterloo. Reade had struggled to support his men, who were in constant fear of gunfire and saber fights, while blinded by smoke from gunpowder, and deafened by cannon blasts. All that day, they had fought, and by evening, the wounded, dead, and dying covered the battleground.

The news that the Allied forces, led by the Duke of Wellington and the Prussian General von Blücher, had defeated Napoleon's Grande Armée brought little peace to Reade as he squatted beside the injured.

Miles, Lord Warren's son, lay mortally wounded by a musket ball. Miles died before they transported him to the infirmary, and they buried him where he lay.

He was only one of many thousands to die that day. So many heartbreaking letters to write. But Reade could never forget bringing the news to Miles's father and helplessly watching hope die in his eyes. It brought back in vivid recall the intense grief of Reade's young self when he lost his mother and his older brother after their yacht sank close to shore.

At ten years old, he'd waded out into the water, but could not reach them and could only watch them drown. The way he had dealt with these memories was to exhaust himself with the work he did for the crown. He closed his eyes, weary to his bones, but knowing sleep was far away.

He never intended to care for Jo. She should marry a suitable man. A calm, even-tempered fellow. That dismal thought led to reflections on how right she felt in his arms, riding home as he'd breathed in the sweet scent of her glorious hair tumbling over her shoulders. She'd been subjected to too much horror, yet her green eyes gazed trustingly into his, and he'd left her with the image of her soft, inviting mouth he longed to kiss.

With a groan, he blew out the candle.

CHAPTER NINETEEN

J O WOKE THE next morning when Sally entered with her cup of chocolate. She had slept in; the mantel clock showed ten o'clock. Beyond the window, the sun shone from a sky of blue. She should feel excited to be alive and ready to tackle a new day, but instead, she was heavy-hearted. Last night she had wanted nothing more than to stay within Reade's arms, but in the cold light of day, she must face facts.

"I was so scared for you, Miss Jo. The staff, too. They waited up for you," Sally said. "Even Mr. Spears. He stayed by the door with your father, even though the footman stood ready to replace him."

"That was sweet of him."

"Yes, your father thanked him."

"I'm pleased, I shall, too."

"A roar went up when you arrived on his lordship's horse. The maids can talk of nothing else this morning."

Jo smiled and nodded. "How kind they all are."

She counted the hours until Reade's visit. At breakfast, her father was full of praise for him. He expressed embarrassment at being taken in by Mrs. Millet, who, after receiving a letter, rushed away and left him midway through the evening.

"I hope she didn't break your heart, Papa," Jo said as he tucked into bacon and eggs.

"There's no fool like an old fool," he said with a sigh. "No, Jo. My

162

heart broke when your mother died. Can't happen again. Mrs. Millet, or Virden, or whatever she calls herself opened an intriguing window into London Society, which I admit I enjoyed. But I've had enough. Your aunt wishes to return home to her cottage and her cats, and I am eager to see Sooty. We'll go just as soon as we've achieved what we came to do. See you and Reade married..."

"But Reade and I aren't getting married, Papa."

He frowned. "You arrived home on Lord Reade's horse with his arms around you. I expected you and him to...."

"No, Papa," Jo said firmly. "Reade rescued me. It is his job, and he's very good at it. I am not about to force him to commit himself because of it."

Her father raised an eyebrow. "I have eyes in my head, Jo. I saw how you two look at each other. Why, it's been Reade this and Reade that since you first laid eyes on him. If we were in Marlborough, the entire village would expect him to marry you."

"But this is London. No one who knows us saw me with him last night. And anyway, he hasn't asked me to marry him." Jo drew in a breath. "Should he do so out of some sense of obligation, I would refuse him."

"Your mother was born into a titled family," her father said with a frown. "It's not because of me, is it?"

"No, Papa."

"If you're sure, my girl. I must assume you know your own mind." He picked up the newspaper and folded it to read an article.

She knew little about the complicated, rather troubled man, but she doubted her father's humble origins would stop Reade. Not if he wanted her. But Letty had warned her. He did not wish to marry. And he had said nothing since to make Jo believe otherwise. How masterfully he'd handled Virden! He would never give that life away to marry her. Nor would he expect her to wait at home for him, wondering if he was dead or alive. Then there was her father to consider. He'd been hurt, his confidence shattered. He'd failed to see through Mrs. Millet's ruse, although the woman had disturbed Jo from their first meeting.

She pushed her scrambled eggs around the plate as her appetite dwindled. Never again would she meet such a man as Reade. And she feared she would never love another man with such passion. All she could think of lying in bed last night was him. The very thought of him sent her blood pounding through her veins. She wanted to draw her fingers through his hair, trace the angles of his aristocratic nose, his lean cheeks, and hard jaw, and allowed herself a moment to think of his sensual lips on hers.

She'd never thought seriously about making love before, beyond a few giggles with her girlfriend. This was desire that settled low in her belly, like a yearning for something she didn't quite understand. Pushing away her half-eaten breakfast, she reached for her cup and sipped without tasting the tea. Best they did not meet again after today. She must try to forget him. "You're right, Papa. We must go home."

"No, my dear," her father said, putting down his newspaper, his about-face surprising her. "You must deal with things head-on and take up the threads of your life again. We will stay until the lease on this house is up. Who knows what might happen in the following weeks?"

"Very well, Papa." Did he think she and Reade...? Or was he hopeful she would meet another suitor? There wasn't room in her heart for anyone else.

Jo hovered over the silver salver on the entry table. Three calling cards. "A busy afternoon. Several gentlemen wish to pay their respects, Miss Dalrymple," Spears said with a warm smile.

"It would seem so, Mr. Spears." Jo's heart sank as she sifted through them. Two gentlemen, she had danced with at her last ball, the other she had met at the picnic in Richmond. How annoying. They might be here when Reade called.

"WHAT HAPPENED AT the Home Office?" Cartwright asked Reade as they ate luncheon in one of Reade's favorite restaurants. "I admit to relief at not being dragged into this one."

"Everyone expressed relief the matter is at an end. We have notified the Regent."

"His majesty should reward you. Another title, more lands?"

Reade grinned. Cartwright lifted Reade from the grim mood he found himself in. "Prinny wants the whole thing brushed under the carpet. He has banished Lothian to the Continent for two years. Rivenstock isn't so lucky. He will suffer the full force of the law. Mrs. Millet has disappeared. It's believed she's escaped to Scotland."

Cartwright whistled softly. "Will you send someone after her?"

"I am tempted. It would need to be someone adept at stealth. The Scots might object."

"And Miss Dalrymple? Is marriage in the wind?"

Reade cocked a brow at his friend's audacity. "Best she chooses another man."

Cartwright put down his cutlery to observe him. "Mind telling me why?"

"She's a beautiful, trusting soul, Jo."

"Which means?"

"She deserves the best."

"Something better than a war hero? Have you forgotten how many lives you saved when your superb tactics outwitted the French in Spain?"

Reade sat back and scowled, hoping to dissuade him from continuing. It didn't work.

"You don't love the lady?" Cartwright persisted.

"Love doesn't come into it. Leave this alone, I beg you."

"All right," Cartwright said with a sigh. "I might ask Letty to talk to you, however."

Reade lowered his head in his hands. He laughed. "Not if you're my friend, you won't."

"I'll say only this," Brandon said seriously. "You blame yourself unfairly for what happened in the past. You have just saved two young women's lives and numerous others. I believe that counts for a great deal, don't you?"

Reade studied his friend's intense face. What he didn't say had more weight than his words. Reade had failed to save young Miles, but because he had a duty to all his men, that wasn't possible. Nor could he have saved his mother and Bart. And perhaps there was never anything he could have done to appease his father for being the wrong son to survive.

Tension he hadn't been aware he carried eased from his body. Reade rubbed his neck; he'd be a fool to turn his back on a chance at love. Did Jo want him? Was it love or gratitude she felt for him?

He nodded. "Thank you, Brandon. You're the best friend a man could have."

Cartwright nodded. "And don't you forget it."

Reade laughed and pushed back his chair. "I must now go to see Dalrymple, who seems to have warmed to me, somewhat."

And Jo, he wanted to see her.

CHAPTER TWENTY

T HE THREE GENTLEMAN callers crowded the drawing room. Jo's
father had not appeared, leaving her and Aunt Mary to entertain
them.

Jo had been determined to hide her feelings from Reade, but when
he walked into the parlor and their gazes locked, her resolve crumbled,
and she struggled not to rush to him.

"How nice to see you, Lord Reade. My father wishes to speak to
you after tea," was all she could manage.

"Yes, of course." Reade chose the last remaining seat, a straight-
backed chair. He shifted about, looking uncomfortable.

Aunt Mary, with an adoring expression, fussed about him. She
poured his tea and offered him the cake platter.

Reade, a napkin on his knee, sipped his tea while talking about cats
with her aunt. His cat, Alistair, an excellent mouser, lived at his
property in the north.

The three gentlemen eyed each other with raised eyebrows, and as
soon as was polite to do so, took their leave.

Jo struggled not to giggle. Reade, so large he made the room look
smaller, forked up pieces of cake while discussing the different breeds
and personalities of felines. She sought his gaze, expecting to find
laughter in his eyes, but they were dark and unfathomable.

Her aunt was expressing her heartfelt thanks and her joy at having her niece safe. While Reade demurred, her father came in and added his effusive thanks to her aunt's.

While many questions were asked of him, Reade revealed few details about how matters now stood with the criminal gang, except to say Mrs. Millet had fled to Scotland. This silenced her father, and they said nothing more about Jo's narrow escape, for which she was thankful. After a maid removed the tea tray, her father stood and cast a glance at Aunt Mary. "If you'll excuse us, my lord, Miss Hatton and I must speak to the staff. A problem below stairs."

Her father's intention was so obvious, Jo flushed. When they left the room, Reade moved to sit beside her on the sofa. He took her hand in his, folding his long fingers around hers, making her pulse race. "Have you recovered from your ordeal, Jo?"

"Completely," she said, smiling brightly. She wondered if he would go after Mrs. Millet. She couldn't see him leaving the matter unresolved. "We have received so many invitations, I declare the Season will be dreadfully busy. Shall we see you at Lady Jersey's soiree?"

He released her hand. "Unfortunately, no. I'm to accompany the Regent to Brighton tomorrow. I am on the way to see him now."

She was unlikely to see him again, she thought with dreadful clarity. "Then, I mustn't keep you. Brighton is a place I'm yet to visit. I've never seen the sea, only in paintings." She was talking too fast and looked at her hands, unable to meet his searching gaze.

"Perhaps you should rest awhile. You've been through a lot, Jo. Things a young woman should never see. Virden's death…"

"I'm made of sterner stuff than you might think," she blurted. "And will always be eternally grateful to you, Reade. One day I will tell my children how bravely you saved their mother."

He frowned. "Has an offer been made?" He smiled. "Not one of those three, I gather."

She forced her lips into a smile. "No, Papa deals with anything of that nature. He has my best interests at heart."

He stood abruptly. "Then I might wish you happy soon."

She came to her feet and curled her fingers into her palms, not to reach out to him. To tell him this was all nonsense. That there would be no one for her but him. That she loved him. But would he want to hear it?

"I must go." He shrugged and smiled. "The Regent awaits."

"Of course." She bobbed, ducking her head, afraid her face would give her away. "I hope your journey to Brighten is pleasant."

"Thank you, Jo," he said, his voice a low rumble. "Please give my regards to Charlotte when next you see her."

"She will want to thank you herself, Reade."

"That's entirely unnecessary. When I return from Brighton, I shan't be in London long for matters await me in the north."

With a small bow, he left her.

Jo ran to the window and watched him enter a carriage. Sobs tore at her throat. Her chest heaving, she ran upstairs, fearing her father or Aunt Mary might see her. She didn't want to worry them. And especially her father, who had been hopeful Reade would ask for her hand.

Sally paused, tidying away clothes. "Oh, Miss Jo. What has upset you so?"

"He doesn't love me, Sally. I was foolish to think he would cast himself at my feet and promise to give up his work for the crown."

"Perhaps he doesn't know you care about him?"

Jo pulled out her handkerchief and dabbed her eyes. "I didn't think it fair. He might have felt pressured."

Sally's eyebrows shot up. "Lord Reade? I doubt anyone could pressure him into doing anything he didn't wish to do."

"But he could have spoken. He didn't."

"With all those gentlemen calling on you?"

The undeniable and dreadful facts remained. "He wouldn't give up his government position for me. I wouldn't ask it of him, but I would hate it, Sally, wondering if he had been hurt, or worse."

"Oh, miss. You look so upset. Let me help you into bed, and I'll bring you a hot drink."

"Yes. I think I will." As she undressed, Jo felt exhausted and more miserable than she'd ever been in her life.

"Thank you, Sally. I am grateful to have you with me." Jo pulled the coverlet over herself. She dabbed her eyes. In a tree outside her window, a bird fed its fledglings. Spring would soon pass into summer, and before she knew it, they would go home. The stark realization of all that entailed brought on a fresh bout of tears.

As THE ROYAL coach took Reade and the Prince Regent to Brighton, Reade arrived at the painful acceptance that some lucky devil would snatch Jo up. Providing her sharp-eyed father approved of him. He'd just better deserve her. Reade had never experienced jealousy. Didn't think himself capable of the emotion. Why he felt a twinge now when he hadn't even taken Jo to bed was beyond him. More than a twinge, he decided, folding his arms with a frown.

"You appear not quite yourself, Reade," Prinny observed, surprising him. The Regent seldom noticed other people's moods, as the world revolved around himself. "It's this unpleasant business you've had to deal with." He shrugged. "Such things go on. But to have it touch one's own family is beyond belief. The matter is at an end. Roland will kick up his heels in France until I permit him to come home. Let him get up to his tricks over there. I am eager to show you the renovations to the Pavilion."

"I look forward to it, Your Highness."

"Nash has improved on Holland's plan by replacing the north and south end bays with pavilions to create music and banquet rooms…" Prinny went on.

"A brilliant example of industrial progress, and the arts, Your Highness," Reade said when called upon to make a comment.

"Quite so," Prinny said, jutting out his chin. "It is said that my grand banquet held in January for the Grand Duke Nicholas of Russia was the grandest of all time. Antonin Careme created over one hundred dishes for it. A terrible pity you missed it."

"It was. My father's illness prevented my attendance, Your Highness."

"Yes. Most unfortunate. And his subsequent passing. Ah, here we are!"

CHAPTER TWENTY-ONE

C HARLOTTE SAT WITH Jo at the Duchess of Walbrook's ball. "I've been hoping to see Lord Reade. Mrs. Lincoln wishes to thank him."

"He might be away at his country estate." Jo had looked for him at every social event in the last three weeks.

"Mr. Lambton called on me and Mrs. Lincoln yesterday for the third time," Charlotte said, excitement sparkling in her eyes. "I believe we might suit."

Jo smiled. "Oh, Charlotte, I do hope so. You like him?"

"I do. He's sober-minded. And kind, I think. Mrs. Lincoln is confident he'll propose. She has written to my grandfather."

"I am thrilled for you."

"Thank you, Jo. I expected to hear news of your engagement before this."

"I've met no one I want to marry. My father wishes to return home to Marlborough, but he refuses to leave London until my future is settled."

"I expected it to be Lord Reade. The way you danced together. You looked like a couple." She sighed. "It will be a lucky woman who marries him.

Jo studied the fan in her hands. "He doesn't appear to want to marry."

"Do many gentlemen? Most wait until they're forced by age or circumstances."

Jo's shoulders heaved in a sigh. "But never love?"

"Rarely, I imagine," Charlotte said pragmatically. "Mr. Lambton is as practical as I am. We have clear ideas for the future."

Jo's spirits lowered. She was usually such a cheerful person, seldom down for long. But she'd been struggling to present a happy demeanor of late, which hadn't fooled her father.

"They've called a country dance." Charlotte rose. "Let me know if you spy Lord Reade among the crowd."

"I will, Charlotte." Jo doubted Reade would be here tonight. Even if he was in London, he rarely appeared at these affairs. She arranged her stiff features into a smile of welcome as her next partner approached her.

The gentleman trod twice on her slippers and smelled of camphor. She could not quit the set until the dance ended, or not dance again tonight. And there was always the chance that Reade might come. When she returned to her seat after the set, Letty joined her. "You don't seem your bright self, Jo."

"A little tired, perhaps, Letty." Jo wondered if Cartwright had told her about the Virdens.

"I have sent an invitation to my soiree on Saturday to you. I confess the party to be a sudden whim of mine. I hope you can come at such short notice."

"We aren't engaged elsewhere and should love to come."

"They called the waltz." Letty patted Jo's hand and stood as her husband emerged from the crowd.

Jo did not waltz, but sat watching her friends with envy.

When the next dance was called, she steeled herself to dance with a gentleman who always seemed to look down his nose at her. She smiled politely, prepared to endure a dance that only brought comparisons to Reade to mind.

It had become too difficult to remain in London. No man would ever measure up to Reade or claim her heart. And she refused to settle for second best. She must try to convince her father to take her home.

BEYOND THE WINDOW, the sky was a limitless blue. Reade tucked into his breakfast ham and eggs. He'd discovered something surprising since he'd arrived at Seacliffe. His nightmares had ceased, and he slept each night soundly. He looked around the castle with fresh eyes and a new sense of belonging. It wasn't the improvements, the oak paneling polished in the great hall, the bright carpets laid over stone floors in the salon, or the rich damask curtains at the windows, although they pleased him. Nor was it visiting his tenant farmers and discussing his stock with his steward, a splendid fellow, although he enjoyed all of it. This went deeper, to his very soul.

He hadn't worked for the crown for money, or praise, for that was rare in this business. And he didn't do it just for the excitement, like some. Reade considered his experience of war enabled him to be of use to the government. Perhaps he was still fighting a war of sorts, this time against evil. And when evil threatened to destroy the good, he took up the challenge. But he wanted a different life for himself now. He would write a letter of resignation when he returned to London.

Two days ago, as the sea wind, cool and salt-laden, washed over him, he strolled the shore. He watched the gulls dip and soar overhead in the blue-gray sky, and the eternal waves break onto the rocks. His thoughts were not about the sadness that had crippled him for too long in the past, but the future, and with it came the beginnings of hope. Something was missing here to give his home a heart and make him whole. A position only a certain feisty redhead could fill. Would she have him? Or had he deliberated too long and lost her to another man?

The post brought a letter from Cartwright. A loquacious missive from a man normally of few words. Politics and gossip-filled both pages. And then a surprising penultimate sentence. Miss Dalrymple was still in London and not yet engaged. Although several gentlemen remained hopeful, the lady was earning a reputation for being cold.

Cold? What nonsense. Jo was a passionate soul. The letter brought him hope. Was he to continue living a half-life? Or do as Cartwright suggested and take a chance on love? Reade pushed away his plate and called for his valet to pack.

They left for London before luncheon.

Three days later, arriving back at his rooms in Albany, he sat at his desk and went through the post. An invitation to Letty's soiree the following night was among them. Reade sensed this had something to do with Brandon's letter. Were his friends trying to bring them together? He expected to find Jo at the soiree.

Had he been a fool and left it too late? Letty would surely know if Jo had met someone. He drank his coffee and began a letter to his solicitor. The lease on his townhouse had expired. He'd initially planned to lease it again but now changed his mind. The house required renovation; the lord knew what condition it was in. He hadn't lived there since he was a boy. That done, he went out to get his hair cut, and thence to Gentleman Jackson's boxing studio to let off a bit of steam. And then he would seek Cartwright at his club to accept the invitation.

CHAPTER TWENTY-TWO

J O TOOK EXTRA care with her appearance for the Cartwright's soiree in Grosvenor Square. She wore the white and gold evening gown with her gold locket and gold slippers, and Sally had become adept at arranging Jo's hair in the current fashion.

The butler admitted them to the drawing room where some forty guests stood drinking champagne. A gentleman played Chopin at the pianoforte. Jo searched unsuccessfully for Reade. He might still be in the country. Letty, in a silk gown the color of strawberries, came with Cartwright at her side to welcome them.

"I'm so pleased you could come. We have some interesting guests here tonight. Sarah Siddons, the great tragedienne, has promised to delight us with a reading. She appears so seldom now since she retired."

"How wonderful," Jo murmured. Perhaps she should pinch herself. "The cream of the *ton* were here tonight." Jo took a glass of champagne from a footman, her gaze roaming the long, elegant room. Lord Liverpool was engaged in conversation with Lady Jersey. "They make me a little nervous."

An hour passed while the guests engaged them in conversation before Letty joined Jo on one of a pair of cream satin and gilt sofas. "So, Jo, how are you, really?"

"I am fine, thank you." Jo wondered if Letty had heard the gossip.

She must have. It appeared in a popular scandal sheet. Jo rebuffed all offers. It suggested she had no wish to marry and accused her of being cold-hearted. It made her all the keener to leave London. Her nerves suffered, and it was difficult to refute the gossip because there was a cold-core lodged in her heart.

"Good to see you, Lord Reade," a gentleman's voice came from behind Jo's sofa. "I hear you are off to Scotland, sir."

Jo's frisson of delight at hearing his name faded with the realization that he was going to find Mrs. Millet. Her fingers trembled around the glass, and she spilled droplets on her gloves.

Reade came into view, tall and imposing in his black evening clothes, and so handsome, her heart gave a leap. "Allow me." He produced a handkerchief and offered it to her with a smile.

"Thank you." Struggling to regain her composure, she dabbed at the almost invisible droplets.

"It is good to see you again, Miss Dalrymple."

"And you, Lord Reade." She held out his handkerchief.

He returned it to his pocket and greeted his hostess, who hovered with an enigmatic smile. "Letty."

"Good of you to come, Reade. You have not been long in Town, Cartwright tells me."

"I returned as soon as I heard you were to hold one of your legendary soirees," he said with a bow.

"Charmer," Letty said with a laugh.

Cartwright shepherded Jo's father and aunt over to the door. She heard him mention a first edition in the library.

A guest appeared at Letty's elbow, and she excused herself. For a moment, Jo and Reade were alone. He sat beside her.

"Was your journey north successful?" she asked.

His dark eyes searched hers. "It was. I don't like those shadows beneath your eyes, Jo," he murmured. "Are you well?"

"I'm...I'm..." Jo's lips trembled, and she feared she would cry. She loved him so much. Mrs. Millet would have friends, treacherous ones. Jo couldn't bear to think of him in danger again. It was impossible not to love him. But he was restless. He would not choose a contented, quiet country life. And she was hopelessly ordinary. A baroness? How absurd. As if he would want her.

She couldn't bear it a moment longer. "I suppose I am more tired than I thought."

"Jo..."

She busied herself with her fan. "The last two weeks have been a whirlwind of engagements and callers."

His dark brows drew together. "You are engaged?"

"My daughter is not engaged, Lord Reade," her father said at her elbow. "There have been offers, and she has refused them."

People turned, and conversations paused.

Oh, Papa, Jo thought, they will laugh at you. "I have developed a headache, Papa," she said faintly, which was true, her temples thumped. "I wonder if you'd take me home?"

Reade had risen to his feet. He said no more, but he watched with concern as they made their apologies to the Cartwrights.

"A pity to Miss Sarah Siddons' performance, but no matter," Aunt Mary said in the carriage. "As long as you are all right, Jo."

"I've ruined your evening," Jo said, trembling with distress.

"Nonsense," her father said. "You've saved me from Siddons. I am not a devotee. It would bore me witless."

"Does your head hurt terribly, Jo?" Aunt Mary sighed. "You must take Feverfew and go straight to bed."

"It does a little," Jo said guiltily. "The pace of London does not agree with me. I would like to return to Marlborough, Papa."

"If you wish, Jo. But I'm disappointed. Lord Reade..."

"He is about to go to Scotland."

"Is he? Can't say I'm sorry to leave London, but I think it regrettable about the baron. I have great respect for him and rather hoped...well, never mind."

Jo stared at him. "I thought you disliked him, Papa."

"Not at all. He is the perfect husband for you, my girl. He would look after you. Keep you safe. You have a propensity to go off on tangents, you know. Why there was that time when you…"

Jo didn't hear the rest. She had pushed Reade away. And yet when she looked into his eyes, she had known he cared for her. When had she become such a coward?

EXASPERATED, READE SAT in his drawing room with his boots resting on a table, a whisky in his hand. The evening had been worked out in advance like a military campaign. But any campaign run along those lines would have been an abject failure. He had left Brandon and Letty as confused as he was. When he'd told them of his intention to ask Jo to marry him, both expressed delight. Brandon offered to keep the library empty of guests while Letty brought Jo to Reade there where they could be alone.

In those first few minutes, when Jo turned toward him, he could have sworn he saw something akin to love in her eyes. And then she rushed away as if the place was on fire. What was he to make of it? He admitted to his shortcomings in matters of the heart, as Cartwright would no doubt remind him, given a chance. His love life had been far less complicated in the past. He supposed because he'd never cared deeply for anyone. And it now seemed that his life depended on Jo being in it.

He downed the whisky. He wasn't about to go to Scotland, Lord Derringham had it wrong, but maybe he should. Take the bit between his teeth again. Find Mrs. Verdin before she created havoc and damaged more lives. But the prospect held no attraction for him. The whisky tasted sour in his mouth, and he put the glass down.

CHAPTER TWENTY-THREE

D EEPLY DESPONDENT, JO sat at the breakfast room table alone, sipping her tea, the toast cooling on the plate. There was nothing for it now but to go home to Marlborough.

The butler entered the room with a parcel. "Good morning, Mr. Spears," Jo said. "As you see, we are preparing to return home."

"This was delivered this morning," he held the small package out to her. I'll be sorry to see you go, Miss Dalrymple," he said, surprising her. "Serving Lord Pleasance is somewhat monotonous, but please don't quote me on that." His ordinarily, dour face broke into a smile.

Jo grinned.

There was no return address on the box. "Who can have sent it?" she said, finding herself alone, as Mr. Spears had tactfully withdrawn.

Pulling the paper off the small box, she opened it.

"Oh!" Her heart beating madly, she picked up the perfect, soft white feather. She held it to her cheek for a moment and then leaped to her feet and dashed into the hall to call for her bonnet. Mr. Spears opened the front door for her, and Jo flew down the steps, tying the strings as she went.

The sun was warm on her back as she ran several blocks to the park. Jo was short of breath by the time she reached the corner of Upper Brook Street and Park Lane. She dodged a carriage and crossed the road. Before she reached the gate, Reade ran to meet her.

"Jo! My love!" He looked in the direction she'd come. "You're alone? Why didn't you bring Sally?"

"I didn't think…" she frowned up at him. "Are you cross with me?"

"Oh, Jo! How could I be when you are here and looking so beautiful?" He lifted her up, his hand on her waist and kissed her, startling a lady walking her dog.

He set her back on her feet. "Will you marry me, Jo?"

She had wanted to hear those words from his lips so much she thought she would cry. "Yes, Reade."

"My name is Gareth, sweetheart."

"Gareth," she said shyly, although she already knew his given name, having made a point of discovering it weeks ago. "I have to confess that your work will worry me. But I mustn't complain, you are so very good at it."

His arms tightened around her, and he drew her close, his mouth grazed her earlobe. "Jo, darling," he murmured. He framed her face in his hands and kissed her. Jo's breath left her in a rush. She reached up to pull him closer and knocked off his hat, threading her fingers through the silky hair at his nape.

Reade released her, and with a laugh, stooped to pick up his hat. He tucked her arm into his elbow, and they walked along the path.

"I've lost my taste for the work, Jo."

"You aren't going to Scotland in search of Mrs. Millet?"

"No, the gentleman was mistaken."

"You haven't decided this for my sake?"

He turned to look at her. "So I may spend my days and nights with you? Is that so surprising?" He pushed back her bonnet and kissed her lightly on the lips again. "Visiting my estate was different this time. It felt right for the first time in a long time. I want to live there, but only if you'll live there with me."

She frowned; there was one last sticking point.

"What troubles you?" He pinched her chin gently. "Don't you like to live in the country? There's always the London Season."

"Oh, yes. I want a farm like my father's with chickens and ducks."

He laughed. "We have fowl plenty at the farm."

"It's my father," Jo said uneasily. "I don't want him to be alone. He has no one now that Aunt Mary plans to move into her new cottage."

"Then, he must live with us."

"It worries me a little. Papa's ways are different. I should not like the *ton* to offend him. Some can be cruel."

"Have they offended him?"

"He hasn't said so."

"After he left last night, a guest inquired after him. He's popular with some, you know."

She widened her eyes. "Papa is popular?"

"Yes. He's plain speaking. It might surprise you, but many people approve of him. Down to earth commonsense isn't so common in the upper echelons of Society."

She laughed. "I suppose it isn't."

"Your papa is knowledgeable about a number of things. He's had a more adventurous life than most."

"He served under Admiral Nelson at Agamemnon," Jo said with a rush of pride.

Reade smiled and brushed a hand softly across her cheek. "He didn't seem to approve of me, initially. I hope that is no longer the case, as I must ask him for your hand."

"That was because of something Mrs. Millet told him."

"And what was that?"

She didn't want to tell him, fearing it would upset him. "It doesn't matter now."

"It does. You must give me the chance to defend myself."

"She said you left a woman at the altar who was expecting your baby."

Reade looked thunderous. "Wretched woman. A complete fabrication."

"I never believed it for a moment," Jo said in a rush. "I know now why she said it. She wanted to turn my father against you and push her son forward."

He smoothed a lock of hair that had escaped to blow across her cheek. "You've come without a pelisse, and the wind is cool. Shall we walk back?"

"I hadn't noticed the breeze." She was warm down to her toes. "Let's hurry home. Papa will be so pleased, and everyone will want to hear our news."

He raised his eyebrows with a smile. "Everyone?"

"Sally tells me the staff is used to serving a sedate older gentleman and find us of great interest. Even the butler, Mr. Spears, has become our friend."

Reade laughed.

DALRYMPLE WAS PLEASED. He shook Reade's hand and agreed to contact his solicitor to arrange the signing of the marriage settlement. The size of Jo's dowry surprised Reade.

"And you shall come and live with us, Papa," Jo said. "Lord Reade has a large house."

Her father raised ginger eyebrows, his green eyes wide with surprise. "Nothing of the sort, my girl. You and Reade need time alone."

"There's no need for that, sir." Reade grinned. "It's a sizeable place. We might not run into each other from morning till night."

Dalrymple chuckled. "That's as may be. And I appreciate your invitation. But I am eager to return home to Marlborough. It's where I'm most contented. A man knows where he belongs, Lord Reade, and for me, it's where my friends and neighbors are."

"But, Papa..."

Her father shook his head. "Now, Jo, Mrs. Laverty must miss our card games. And I confess I miss them, too."

"The invitation remains open, sir," Reade said. "If you change your mind."

"You must come for a visit before the winter makes travel too difficult, Papa," Jo said.

"We shall come. Mary, too, and perhaps Mrs. Laverty might enjoy the trip."

"Oh, Papa! That would be wonderful."

"Don't get your hopes up, Jo. Leave a fellow to organize his own life. I look forward to seeing your home farm, Reade."

"I will benefit greatly from your sage advice, sir."

After luncheon, Jo saw Reade to the door. The butler cleared his throat and made for the servants' stairs. Left alone, he gathered her into his arms and hugged her. "I can't believe my good fortune," he said huskily. "Come outside with me."

She took his hand, and they walked down the steps. "What is it? You look so somber. You are happy?"

"Blissfully, my love. But there is something I need to say now before we go any further."

"You're going to Scotland."

"No." He put a finger to her lips. "I have had trouble...sleeping, since the war. Nightmares. They can plunge me into the doldrums. I'm not always the happiest of fellows. You need to be aware of what you're taking on with me, Jo."

"Oh, my darling." Jo reached up to touch his cheek. "My father told me how troubled the men he served with were after the war. We shall deal with it together."

He hated the thought of seeming weak in her eyes. It twisted his gut. But he didn't hate it enough to give her up. Not when she gazed so tenderly at him that he wanted to kiss her. Aware some of the maids were watching through the iron fence, he settled his hat on his head. "I believe you are the best antidote for any ailment a man might suffer, sweetheart."

She caught his arm as he turned away. "You make me blissfully happy, Gareth."

There were tears on her cheeks. Hell, he couldn't leave like that, he gently kissed them away. Did he hear a faint cheer from belowstairs?

CHAPTER TWENTY-FOUR

T HEIR WEDDING WAS not a large fashionable affair, which was Jo's preference, and Reade agreed. It took place at a small church in Westminster three weeks after Reade's proposal. The church was unadorned, the only concession, white flowers and ribbons decorating the pews. The servants came dressed in their Sunday best. Mr. Spears abandoned his black for a fawn-colored coat, well-made but patched on the elbows.

The Cartwrights had offered to hold the wedding breakfast at their home.

Reade had received a congratulatory letter from the Prince Regent, who expressed his grievance at him retiring from service. Many friends and those from the government offered their best wishes from the prime minister to the home secretary.

Jo wore a new gown, an apricot sarsnet trimmed with broad Van-dyke lace, her Italian, straw bonnet lined with apricot satin and ostrich feathers. Reade was handsome in a gray tailcoat and dark trousers, and his best man, Cartwright, wore blue. Charlotte, in primrose yellow, was Jo's bridesmaid. She had recently become engaged to Mr. Lambton. While Letty, elegant in azure lace, was her matron of honor.

Aunt Mary wore a new lilac-colored dress and turban made for the occasion, and Jo's father looked very smart in a dark tail-coat with a flower in his buttonhole, but grimaced and tugged at his cravat. He smiled and kissed her as he gave her away. Jo saw that he was sad, and she was glad of Mrs. Laverty.

Once the register was signed, she and Reade emerged onto the street. The servants cheered and threw rice as they laughingly climbed into the landau and drove away.

"Was that Mr. Black standing on the pavement?" Jo asked as they traveled to Grosvenor Square.

"Yes, good of Winston to come."

"Letty mentioned something interesting as she helped me dress."

"Oh?" His appreciative gaze took her in from her bonnet to her shoes. "She did well."

"Did well?" Jo asked, distracted.

"Dressing you."

She giggled.

"But, I shall attend to the undressing."

Jo trembled at the heated look he gave her.

"What did Letty tell you?" he asked, drawing her focus back to what she needed to say.

"Cartwright left the service when they first married, but as you know, works for the crown again."

"Now and again."

She studied his face beneath his tall beaver hat. "Might they draw you back in one day?"

His hand tightened around hers. "Not if you'd rather I didn't, my love."

She frowned. "So, it's to be my decision. That's unfair."

He gave her a silky glance, which made her tremble. When he looked at her like that, her stomach felt heavy and strange. She fought to gather her thoughts. He could distract her with a look!

"Sweetheart, I honestly have no intention of returning to the Home Office. But if something of vital importance occurred and they called upon me, I would have to say yes, would I not?"

She sighed and shook her head at him. He had wriggled out of that far too neatly. She settled within his arm. He was hers now and would be for the conceivable future. That had to be enough. "Charlotte said Anabel Riley came from a small village in West Yorkshire. Do you think we might call in there on our way to Cumbria?"

"You haven't given up on her, I see. I hope we don't find anything to upset you."

"I'll take that chance. We should do all we can to find her."

"I have had the men searching London for Miss Riley for weeks. There's been no sign of her."

"I'm not sure Virden took Anabel. He said the last girl was one his mother enticed off the street."

"Virden wasn't the most truthful of men."

"He didn't have a reason to lie to me."

"No, perhaps not. But this isn't a fitting conversation for today. But I promise we'll call in to her village on our way north. There's always the chance that someone received word from her."

"Thank you, darling."

A smiled quirked the corner of his mouth. "When you look at me like that, I'm happy to do anything you ask."

Jo shook her head, amused. She didn't believe it. He was not a man to be manipulated, which was one of the things she admired about him, so she smiled and leaned her head against his shoulder.

As THE COACH took them to the Cartwright's, Reade had time to dwell on his life. He had not the slightest doubt of how he felt about Jo, his love for her was rooted deep in his soul, but he hadn't entirely trusted the grim moods which ruled him would release him from their grip. He would never forget the appalling bloodshed and loss of life painted in vivid pictures on his memory. He had tried to help the families of the good men in his regiment who shed their blood on the battlefield, and those who returned, often badly injured or maimed and unable to find work. He wanted to do more. Women were often better able to do these things, and he looked forward to discussing it with Jo.

At the wedding breakfast held in the Cartwrights' white and gold ballroom, his eyes rested on her as they danced. He was proud of his enchanting wife, who wasn't just caring of others, but strong and brave. He wanted to whisk her away and have her to himself.

"It has been the very best of weddings." A half-wreath of spring blossom decorated her dark red curls, her big green eyes beneath dark gold lashes a blend of affection and longing which made him catch his breath.

"Yes, indeed," he agreed gravely.

"And I have the bravest and most handsome bridegroom in all of England."

He grinned. "Then I have succeeded in pulling the wool over your eyes."

A dimple appeared at the corner of her mouth. "You shall not convince me otherwise."

He sighed. "May you always stay that way, my Jo. I love you so much. Shall we go soon?"

Jo turned in his arms to look around the long room. A trio played a Mozart piece, and other dancers had joined them on the floor. Her Aunt Mary and her father chatted with guests. "I feel like I belong to all this," Jo said, with a misty smile. "For the first time."

"A notice appeared in *The Morning Post*."

"I wonder if my mother's family in Marlborough will see it. They have never welcomed me because, in their eyes, my father wasn't good enough for them."

"Class is not always a matter of birth," Reade said.

"Virden thought it was. That he hadn't been born on the right side of the blanket consumed him."

He frowned. "Jo."

"Yes?"

"I won't have mention of them here or during our honeymoon. Or, in fact, at any time. That's in the past, Jo. And there it will remain."

"But if we could just find Anabel, I shall not speak of it again."

"I can see it will be up to me to distract you," he said, his gaze capturing hers. "I am eager for the task."

The smile she bestowed on him was as intimate as a kiss. His arm tightened around her. Loving Jo was going to be a blissful adventure.

CHAPTER TWENTY-FIVE

IT WAS JO'S first sight of Reade's townhouse. She'd been unable to visit because painters and decorators were at work. Its magnificence rivaled that of the Cartwrights' home. A footman opened the door, and she stepped with Reade onto the black-and-white marble tiles of the foyer. A return staircase curved away to the upper floors, where a crystal chandelier hung from the lofty ceiling.

Reade took her hand and led her across Aubusson carpets, through beautiful reception rooms hung in silk and decorated with brocade and velvets. A fresh smell of paint lingered. "I hope the décor meets with your approval," he said, glancing at her. "I left the improvements to the decorators, as I know little of such things."

Jo smiled. It mattered little to him. He'd done this for her. He would entertain with her in this beautiful drawing room, but she suspected he would rather be out of doors, riding his horse. She smiled. "How could I not? It's a beautiful house."

"Shall we go upstairs? You'll want to change."

Sally was at the trunk in the boudoir, as Jo entered. The maid came into the bedchamber, her face wreathed in smiles. She had been overjoyed when Jo told her she would continue as her maid.

"I'll wear the blue cambric, Sally."

"Yes, Miss Jo."

Jo drew in a breath. The elegant furnishings and superb artworks had stunned her the minute she stepped through the door. She'd never acquainted the man she knew with such wealth and grandeur.

When dressed, she came down to the drawing room hung with paintings and huge gilt-edged mirrors. She wandered out onto the terrace to inspect the walled garden of trees and clipped shrubs. In the lane behind was the stables where Reade's beloved horse Ash was stalled.

With a smile, Reade came to join her. She reached up to order his glossy locks. They were faintly damp. When he slipped an arm around her waist and hugged her to his side, she breathed in his familiar masculine smell, which never failed to arouse her. "It's not much of a garden," he said. "I prefer the wildness of Seacliffe."

Jo understood now why he'd preferred to live at Albany. Rattling around this house on his own would be anathema to him. Was it because of his years in the army he preferred a simple life? Or just the man he was? Jo had many questions, but she wasn't impatient. They had all the time in the world.

After a light repast in the dining room, it was still daylight when they made their way upstairs. Jo was a little breathless. She didn't consider herself to be shy, but she wanted so much to please him.

He left her to go to his bedchamber. Jo entered to bathe and change into the negligee she'd recently purchased. This was nothing like her usual white lawn nightgowns. The pale green silk trimmed with ribbons and lace clung and revealed much of her body.

After Sally brushed out her hair, she left her.

Jo looked at the enormous bed. There were steps to reach it. She slid down on smooth, fresh sheets beneath the covers and lay examining the gold tent of fabric above her, her heart thumping as she listened for the door to Reade's apartment to open.

When he appeared in a dressing gown, she sat up, clutching the sheet to her chest. His gaze sought hers as he crossed the carpet. He stood before her with that special smile he had for her, which had always made her feel safe. She didn't feel so safe now; at the serious intent in his eyes, a euphoric rush of pleasure and anticipation made her sink down with a gasp.

He kicked off backless slippers, his hands at his dressing gown belt. Jo eyed the vee of smooth, lightly tanned skin and the smattering of dark, crisp curls at his throat. Beneath the midnight blue silk, he appeared to be naked. She quivered. "This is a very high bed," she said in a rush, with a need to defuse the tension.

Reade's hand stilled on the belt. "Is it?"

"A robber could hide under there."

One eyebrow rose, and his lips parted on a grin. "Would you like me to look?"

"That's unnecessary, surely," Jo said as her fingers gathered the sheet to her chin.

"I am always happy to please a lady."

As he lifted the coverlet to peer beneath the bed, Jo was overcome with giggles.

With a laugh, Reade shrugged off his dressing gown and joined her beneath the covers. A large warm body lay against hers, and a broad hand settled on her hip. "The only one you must contend with tonight, Jo, is me." He kissed her lightly on the lips. "And I will be gentle."

The mere glimpse of his naked body made her yearn to lift the covers. But Reade distracted her by untying the ribbons at her throat. He drew the silk away, and murmuring her name, gathered her to him. His masculine aroma teased at her. With her breasts crushed against his body, all satiny skin, sinew, muscle, and bone, her anxiety faded away. This was Reade, her husband, and she loved him. Her arms went around his neck to draw his face down to hers.

"You're lovely, Jo."

His mouth sought and demanded a response, kissing, nibbling, and lightly biting her lips. With a low, deep sound in his throat, his tongue teased her lips apart and thrust deep into the cavern of her mouth. Shocked at the intimacy, Jo moaned as a throb of yearning began low in her belly. He tasted of sweet champagne. Reade threw off the covers.

She barely noticed when her nightgown landed on the floor.

"You're beautiful, Jo."

He was magnificent. She had to touch him, running her hands over warm skin as muscles rippled across his back and arms. His proud member pressed against her stomach, and his long legs tangled with hers.

Reade teased, tantalized, and aroused her, circling the crest of a nipple and drawing it into his mouth. He ravished her with his mouth, nibbling, licking, finding places on her body Jo hadn't known were so sensitive or arousing. His hand slid between her thighs, and he slipped a finger inside her.

"Oh!" He gently circled that sensitive part of her, and an urgent need made her oddly restless. On fire with longing, she murmured and clutched his head as he moved down to kiss her belly.

When his mouth replaced his fingers, Jo threw her head back and gasped. She arched against him restlessly, not knowing what she craved, but wanting more.

Reade moved up to join her on the pillows, his hand cupping her sex. Embarrassed at how wet she'd become, she turned her face away.

"Look at me, Jo," he rasped.

Jo turned to gaze into his eyes, which were dark with passion. He parted her legs and shifted over her. His hands on her hips, he raised her to meet him, and she felt him, heavy and blunt at her entrance. He pushed slowly inside. "God, Jo, I love you." he murmured.

One thrust, and he pushed deeper. Jo whimpered at the spark of pain.

The discomfort lessened as he moved. A sense of being one with him possessed her, and as he moved inside her, an urgent need gathered low in her stomach. She pressed kisses on the smooth skin of his neck and shoulder, her fingers stroking over his broad back. The sweet pain made her moan. She abandoned herself to pleasure. *"Please,"* she murmured, although she knew not what she wanted. She locked her legs around him and moved to meet each thrust.

With a groan, his thrusts quickened and carried her along, then caught her up in a rolling explosion of feeling which grew in intensity until she almost couldn't bear it. She cried out his name.

A final groan and a rush of warmth inside her. He stilled, breathing heavily.

Panting, Jo sank back, loose, and floaty. She lost all sense of herself. When she opened her eyes, he smiled down at her.

She gave him a wobbly smile and licked her swollen lips, dismayed that tears had gathered at the corners of her eyes.

He eased himself off her and to the side and reached across to wipe away a tear. "Did I hurt you, sweetheart? It won't hurt again, I promise."

"Only a little, but Gareth, I loved it, I love you."

He leaned on an elbow, a tender expression in his eyes. "I like to hear you say my name."

"Gareth," she said again. "It suits you."

A wry smile raised his lips. "I wish I could tell my mother you approve of it. She chose it from among the family names."

"Will you tell me about your mother?"

A shadow crossed his eyes. "I will soon," he promised. "Not to-night, darling. You need to sleep."

"Yes, I think I will." Her breath and the pounding of her heart had slowed. Her bones seemed heavy. Lying beside his warm side, she couldn't keep her eyes open.

READE WOKE EARLY after a surprisingly deep, peaceful sleep and marveled at the absence of a nightmare. The erotic smell of lovemaking lingered, and he smiled as he recalled their night together. The morning sun peeked through a break in the curtains, reaching golden fingers across the carpet toward the bed. Jo was made for love. She had been a curious and passionate lover. He watched her sleep, her glorious hair spread over the pillow, her body curled trustingly against him.

She had come to London to enjoy the Season and had been thrust into the sordid underbelly of London, her life at stake, and he wanted to make it up to her, to keep her safe and love her.

He considered the day ahead. They were to depart London after breakfast and journey north, stopping at coaching inns for the night. While he was keen for them to reach Seacliffe, there was no need to travel at break-neck speed. They would enjoy a leisurely trip through the countryside decked out in spring finery and put up at the best inns.

Jo stirred and smiled sleepily up at him. "Good morning."

"Good morning." He gathered her warm, inviting body close and kissed her.

A knock came at the door.

"Sally, with my chocolate," Jo murmured.

He groaned and threw back the covers. "We leave in a few hours. I'll leave you to dress."

Jo pouted prettily as she followed him from the bed to don her dressing gown.

She was a naked Venus. Alabaster skin and pale pink nipples, a dark red triangle of hair below the gentle curve of her stomach, and long slim legs. His body stirred, wanting her. "Go away, Sally," he called. "Come back in an hour."

With an inviting smile, Jo toyed with the curls on his chest.

Reade cupped Jo's derriere in his hands and pulled her against his arousal as he kissed her. He drew away to search her eyes. "Shall we, my love?"

She murmured an assent.

Reade picked her up and laid her on the bed. He settled behind her, his hands on her hips and eased into her soft warmth, his fingers kneading her soft bottom. Jo squealed and panted and pushed back against his belly. Reade flipped her over and entered her again, his mouth on hers, their tongues tangling until he came with a roar.

He raised himself on his elbows to smile at her. "That should last me until we reach the coaching inn," he said with a grin. "Although I'm not sure, how do you feel about making love in a carriage?"

Jo laughed. "I rather like the idea."

CHAPTER TWENTY-SIX

JO RAISED HER head from Reade's shoulder and groggily viewed the scene passing by the window. The coach traveled through the rugged Pennine hills, the moors stretching away in a swathe of brilliant green. "You promised to wake me," she said accusingly.

He kissed the tip of her nose. "I hadn't the heart, you look so appealing when you sleep, with just an occasional snore."

She laughed and hit him on the arm. Sitting up, she tidied her hair. "Are we near Holfirth?"

"A few miles to go yet."

"Let's go straight to the church. If there's any news of Anabel, the vicar will know."

He drew her back against him. "Darling, don't be too dismayed if there's been no word."

"I'll try not to," Jo said, but her heart felt bruised. She didn't want to think Virden had sent Anabel to some heathen place and left her to her fate. He'd denied it, but Reade was right, she shouldn't believe anything the evil man said.

A half-hour later, the coach trundled down the hill and entered the busy village. They continued along the road and pulled up outside the gray stone parish church.

When they entered, a young man in a curate's clothing came up the aisle toward them. Warm hazel eyes smiled a welcome. Reade introduced them.

Jo met the smile. "We would like to see the vicar."

"I'm sorry, my lady. The vicar is away. He's not expected back until Tuesday."

"Then perhaps you can help us," Reade said.

"I hope so. I'm the curate here. Donaldson is my name."

"Mr. Donaldson, we are seeking news about one of your parishioners," Reade said. "She came to London for the Season last year but left shortly afterward. A friend is most concerned about her and wishes to know how she fares."

"Who is the lady?"

"Miss Anabel Riley."

Donaldson's eyes widened. He ran a hand through his hair and shook his head.

Icy fingers ran down Jo's spine.

"I am a little surprised," he said. "There's no longer an Anabel Riley." He smiled. "But there is an Anabel Donaldson."

"Mrs. Donaldson?" Jo wondered if she'd misheard him. "Anabel is your wife?"

They shared a smile. "I am. Who is asking after her?"

"Miss Charlotte Graham. They became friends last year. Charlotte became concerned when Anabel disappeared."

"Ah, I see. Regrettable. When Anabel's chaperone died unexpectedly, she was forced to return home. I was most fortunate that she did. If she'd remained long in London, some other lucky fellow would have married her," he said with a chuckle.

Jo laughed.

"May we have the pleasure of meeting Mrs. Donaldson?" Reade asked.

Donaldson shook his head. "I'm afraid not. Anabel isn't here. She's gone to York with her mother. Unless you intend to spend a week here?"

"Unfortunately, we are just passing through," Reade said.

"I am sorry to miss her," Jo said. "Please tell her I shall write to Charlotte, who is soon to marry a Mr. Lambton, and give her your address."

"Anabel will be delighted. It upset her very much to have to leave London in a rush with no time to tell anyone. Nor did she have her friend Charlotte's address." He stood. "I am remiss. May I offer you tea in the rectory?"

"Thank you, but no. My wife and I are eager to reach Cumbria before nightfall."

"Anabel will be sorry to have missed you." Donaldson followed them out of the church into the sunshine. "Godspeed." He raised his hand as they settled in the coach.

The horses leapt forward, and the vehicle rocked its way down the road. Jo snuggled against Reade, and he drew the rug over them.

He kissed the top of her head. "Content now, my love?"

"I am, thank you, darling."

"A happy ending," she said. "I must write to Charlotte, and Papa, and Aunt Mary, tonight."

"Tomorrow, Jo."

She met his ardent brown gaze and smiled mischievously. "Yes, tomorrow."

THEIR SPIRITS LIFTED. They were no longer seeking an answer to the fate of Miss Riley. They laughed and kissed, and they talked. Reade did most of it. His sympathetic bride listened quietly as he told her about his childhood and the tragedy which had changed the course of his life. His father's coldness drew a gasp of surprise from loyal Jo. For a parent not to love their children was anathema to her. That a father didn't love a son like Reade, impossible!

He laughed. "I wasn't lily-white, my love."

"No boy would be. I imagine our sons won't be. But you will love them dearly. And wish the best for them."

"You have a big heart Jo, with room enough for everyone. Not everyone has that capacity."

She nodded thoughtfully. "But you do." She traced the straight line of his nose with a finger. Her feather-light touch across his lips and into the dip in his chin brought her close, and his body stirred. "Your work was all about helping unfortunate people, wanting good to triumph over evil."

He drew her close. She was sensitive and perceptive, his bride. Having her near made him want her. The scent of her skin, her hair, her soft, wide inviting mouth, her essence, and her passion. He took control of himself. "We shall arrive at Seacliffe in an hour or two."

She sat forward, a casual hand on his knee, warm and inviting. "What were you saying earlier about love and a carriage? she asked, smiling mischievously.

He pulled her onto his lap.

"Might be better to show you, darling."

EPILOGUE

I T WAS LATE in the afternoon when the coach passed through the tiny hamlet, which was the coastal village of Seacliffe. A mile farther on, they entered through a grand set of gates.

Jo clung to the windowsill, staring out as they continued along a drive bordered by hedges and trees bent by the wind. A glimmer of deep gray-blue water appeared through the foliage.

"I caught a glimpse of the ocean!" she cried, her pulse racing.

"The Irish Sea."

The coach emerged from the trees, and the gravel drive took them along beside a sweep of lawn. A stone castle complete with turret and towers loomed ahead of them with the backdrop of the sea behind it.

For a moment, Jo couldn't speak, then she turned half laughing, half accusatory. "You didn't tell me it was a castle!"

As the coachman drew the horses to a stop, Reade edged forward on the seat with his hand on the door handle. "You're not disappointed? It's not the neat manor house I know you wanted."

She poked him in the side. "I can't wait to see it."

"Castles are not the most comfortable of residences," he said, turning to help her down. "I have attempted to make it so."

A thin, grizzled man dressed in black opened the enormous oak door with a brass ring in the shape of a lion.

"I trust you had a pleasant journey, Baron."

"We did, thank you, Hyde. This is Lady Reade."

He bowed. "Lady Reade."

Jo doubted she would ever grow used to the title. How did the daughter of a haberdasher arrive at this? "How do you do, Hyde. I plan to ask you a million questions later."

Hyde bowed again. "It shall please me to answer them, my lady."

They entered the soaring-roofed great hall, their footsteps echoing across the stone floors. Reade led her into a smaller chamber with furnishings of blue velvet and gold and an enormous stone fireplace. The furniture was of oak. Bookshelves lined two walls, another wall taken up with windows filled with the sky and sea. A ginger-haired cat with a bushy tail sat curled up on the sofa. It leaped down and stalked over to Reade to rub against his legs. He picked the animal up and held it in his arms.

"So this is Alistair." Jo stroked his soft fur. A vibration rumbled through his body. "He loves you."

"He's close to twenty years old," he said. "You're an old cat, aren't you, Alistair?"

Alistair took umbrage at the reference to his age and leaped down from Reade's arms to stalk out the door.

Jo crossed the brightly patterned Eastern rug. A hand on the damask curtain, she stared out at the windswept expanse of grass leading down to the shore. Birds wheeled about in the sky. She breathed in the salty smell and listened to the roar of the sea. Out on that wind-tossed water, Reade had lost his mother and brother when he'd been just a boy. Compassion for him twisted her heart. She turned to observe him where he stood at her shoulder.

She slipped her hand into his. "How extraordinary this view is. And how perfect a setting for my big Viking."

He chuckled and pulled her onto his lap on a gold velvet wing chair. "I'll take you for a tour of the castle and grounds shortly before it gets dark. And after supper, I believe we will go early to bed."

The next morning, Jo smiled and stretched languidly in the carved oak four-poster bed hung with crimson velvet. Reade had been an insatiable lover last night. She was learning to please him and to take her own pleasure. Her cheeks heated as she recalled their unrestrained passion. He had ridden out to visit the farm and fetch his dogs while she planned her day. After she attended to her letters, she would take a stroll along the shore.

A maid came in with her chocolate.

"Thank you, Maude. I wish to speak to the housekeeper and the staff this morning after breakfast."

"Yes, milady."

Reade's man, Minshull, and Sally were to arrive tomorrow. Until then, Jo would make do herself. She had managed perfectly well in Marlborough. She smiled, remembering how her father hated having a valet. He would love Seacliffe. Was he enjoying his Saturday spent with Mrs. Laverty?

Tying a ribbon around her hair, she hurried to the window at the sound of scattering gravel. Reade rode up the drive. Two hounds, tongues lolling, ran alongside Ash. Jo waved to Reade, then hurried from the room to go down and meet them.

The day had turned blustery and cool. Some hours later, Jo, a shawl wrapped around her shoulders, returned to the house from a stroll along the shore.

Reade was in the library with Mr. Black. The two dogs stretched out over the rug in front of a crackling fire at his feet, while Alistair aloofly viewed them from the window embrasure.

They stood as she entered. "Jo, Black has just returned from Scotland. He brings news of Mrs. Virden."

Jo's heart turned over at the mention of the woman's name she never wanted to hear again. "What news, Mr. Black?" She sat in the armchair Reade had drawn closer to the warmth of the fire.

"It was my intention to bring Mrs. Virden back to London to face justice, my lady, but that has proved impossible."

"She's dead, Jo," Reade said.

"She's died? Was it an illness?"

Black shook his head. "She was found strangled in her bed. The Scots will deal with the investigation."

When Black left, keen to continue his journey, Jo sat quietly with Reade on the sofa.

"I never wanted to feel relief that someone has died, but she was evil. It's an end to the horrible business."

Reade hugged her. "An ending, Jo. And the beginning of our lives together."

About the Author

A USA TODAY bestselling author of Regency romances, with over 35 books published, Maggi's Regency series are International bestsellers. Stay tuned for Maggi's latest Regency series out next year. Her novels include Victorian mysteries, contemporary romantic suspense and young adult. Maggi holds a BA in English and Master of Arts Degree in Creative Writing. She supports the RSPCA and animals often feature in her books.

Like to keep abreast of my latest news? Join my newsletter.
http://bit.ly/1m70lJJ

Blog: http://bit.ly/1t7B5dx
Find excerpts and reviews on my website: http://bit.ly/1m70lJJ
Twitter: @maggiandersen: http://bit.ly/1Aq8eHg
Facebook: Maggi Andersen Author: http://on.fb.me/1KiyP9g
Goodreads: http://bit.ly/1TApe0A
Pinterest: https://www.pinterest.com.au/maggiandersen

Maggi's Amazon page for her books with Dragonblade Publishing.
https://tinyurl.com/y34dmquj

Printed in Great Britain
by Amazon

16695506R00122